MORE
Short Scenes and Monologues
for Middle School Students

INSPIRED BY LITERATURE, SOCIAL STUDIES,
AND REAL LIFE

Dedicated to Malinda,
who is now in middle school.

MHS

MORE Short Scenes and Monologues for Middle School Students

INSPIRED BY LITERATURE, SOCIAL STUDIES, AND REAL LIFE

by Mary Hall Surface

YOUNG ACTORS SERIES

A Smith and Kraus Book

A Smith and Kraus Book
Published by Smith and Kraus, Inc.
177 Lyme Road, Hanover, NH 03755
(888) 282-2881
www.SmithandKraus.com

Book design by Julia Hill Gignoux, Freedom Hill Design
Cover photo provided by the author.

The Library of Congress Cataloging-In-Publication Data
Surface, Mary Hall.
More short scenes and monologues for middle school actors / by Mary Hall Surface. —1st ed.
p. cm. — (Young actors series)
Includes bibliographical references.
Summary: A collection of original scenes and monologues
written especially for middle-school actors.
ISBN 1-57525-560-X
ISBN 978-1-57525-560-6
1. Monologues — Juvenile literature. 2. Dialogues — Juvenile literature. 3. Acting — Juvenile literature. [1. Acting. 2. Monologues] I. Young actors series
PN2080.S87   1999
812'.5408—dc21   99-052457

Contents

Introduction

In my twenty-five years of working for and with young people as a director, playwright, and teacher, I have found that eleven- to fourteen-year-olds bring unrivaled energy to the process of making theater. Indeed, they bring this energy to *everything* because of the chronological conundrum of being neither child nor teenager. One minute they are devoted participants. The next they are unresponsive cynics. Then they are ricocheting off the walls simply because they are twelve or thirteen. Most often, they simply want your serious attention as they wrestle with who they are and with becoming who they will be. Drama provides an ideal wrestling mat for the middle schooler.

What distinguishes this book of short scenes and monologues for this age group from my earlier one is my intention to provide a resource not only for drama teachers, but for teachers of language arts, social studies, and character education as well. I've had extensive opportunities in recent years to integrate drama into the curriculum of middle school classrooms. American history and government, ancient cultures and their mythologies, and even earth science all are brought to three-dimensional, hands-on life in these pages. School counselors will find material that invites students to try on decision making, to explore the consequences of action, and to empathize in the visceral way that only drama can provide. I've seen these scenes in action and they work. Their structure and content will enhance your students' learning and inspire them (and you) to embrace drama as a unique and powerful classroom tool.

And drama teachers will find in this volume what drama teachers have celebrated from my first book — short monologues with clear emotional turning points, short scenes for two and four actors with strong relationships and specific objectives, and short scenes for multiple actors in which the roles have relatively equal weight. I have given your actors material that captures their everyday triumphs and hardest knocks. Just as importantly, I am committed to opening our students' eyes and putting them in the shoes of peoples, cultures, and languages beyond their own. This new volume also acknowledges that the world is not the same now that the century has turned. Our students live with fears that grow not only from the shifting sands of adolescence but from their real concerns for the Earth's future and for a secure world. My hope is that middle schoolers will find an honest and empowering voice in these pages.

In the monologues, I give young actors a specific dramatic moment to play. The character in the monologue has an objective. He or she wants something from his or her unseen partner. For example, a son wants his father's attention, a girl wants her friend's approval, or a boy wants some crucial information. The challenge is to discover what the character will do to get what he or she wants — what tactics he or she will use, how far he or she will go. Too many monologues are overly narrative. These monologues require young actors to build a relationship, to react to what is happening *now*. Most distinctively, each monologue has at least one if not more than one specific emotional turning point (when the character has a realization that clearly takes him or her from one emotional place to another.) This demands that the actor find a range of emotions, even within a short monologue form.

The scenes are designed to enable young actors to

behave truthfully in imaginary circumstances (which, to my mind, is the definition of acting.) Each scene has rich, clear circumstances that the actor must envision, and each has strong wants on the part of each character that he or she must pursue as actively as possible. Many of the scenes set up compelling physical circumstances, such as a soccer lesson, a game of four square, or a flight of birds above the desert. This is to push young actors to realize that the development of the physical life of a scene and a character is of equal importance to "saying the lines." Indeed, some very important story beats in the scenes are wordless. (And all students should find the last wordless moment that concludes each scene and monologue.) Also, the text of the scenes is designed to encourage young actors to look beyond spoken lines to the subtext — the myriad thoughts and feelings "beneath" the words of the character. And the text is rich with images — images that the actor must picture in detail so that a character can have full three-dimensional life. When you understand all that is inside a character, then you know "how to say the line."

The subject matter I have chosen for these monologues and scenes is as diverse as our students. To be sure, much of it is rooted in their everyday world — a world that is complex, challenging, funny, and frightening. While most of the material is realistic, I have crossed into the imaginary and mythological realms as well. (Some of the pieces are inspired by my plays, which have been widely performed on professional, community, and educational stages.) I include this material because it is so appealing to actors in this age group. As importantly, it stretches the young actor to develop nonhuman characters, to imagine themselves to be older (a practice I do not advocate in realistic material) or to stand in someone else's shoes in another place and time.

Just as in my first collection, I hope this book will encourage young actors to make clear, strong choices; to develop characters with vivid physical, emotional and vocal ranges; to build rich, powerful relationships onstage; and to use all their creativity to imagine ways to tell the big stories in these short pieces. May all our work build on theater's most ancient function — to bring us into a space where we can imagine together.

Mary Hall Surface
Washington, D.C.
August 2006

The author wishes to acknowledge Marisa Smith; Kevin Reese; Kate Bryer, Richard Bradbury, and the students of Imagination Stage, Bethesda, Maryland; Clayton Doherty, Sarah Barker, and the students of Carpe Diem Summer Theatre Academy, Stratford-upon-Avon, England; Stephen, Rachel, James ("Chippy"), and Miriam Butt; Mary Osterman, Laurie Young, Margo Swire, Lara Estomin, Pamela Carpousis, Barbara Clements, Charlie Abelman, Scott Cartland, and the students of Janney Elementary School, Washington, D.C.; my after-school Shakespeare students; Alison, Todd and Skye Stansbury; Caleb and Anna Fechtor; Marilee Miller at Anchorage Press and Gayle Sergal at Dramatic Publishing for their support of my work and this book; David Maddox for our collaboration on the five musicals listed in the Play Sources; and Malinda Reese and her friends for being a constant source of inspiration.

CHAPTER ONE

Monologues for Young Women
(One minute or less)

SOPHIE

(Talking to her dad.)

You saw what happened, Dad. He bucked! Like some wild
rodeo horse! I halted because that's what the judge said to
do before the last jump. *(Quoting the horse show judge.)*
"Take the last jump at a trot." Chestnut hates that! He
wants to canter — always. But "OK," I said and gave
Chestnut all the right signals. Then he threw me halfway
across the course. Dad, I can tell what you're thinking.
That this is all about the trophy. It's not! No, it's a worse
feeling than losing. Much worse! See . . . I don't know if
there's something wrong with Chestnut or with me. Was it
something I did? I know that horse and he knows me.
Better than most *people* do. Why couldn't he understand
me? How could it go so wrong? If things aren't right
between Chestnut and me, how can anything be right.

ARIEL

(Talking to her friend, Lana.)

Why is everybody so worried about me, Lana? I *like* to be by myself. I *like* my own company. Isn't that what everybody wants from a preteen? Our teacher is always telling us to be self-confident. And my mom tells me to be "true to myself" every other minute. Well, myself likes to be alone. See how I've decorated my room? Postcards from every cool place I've ever been. Did you see my mountain of stuffed animals? My shelf full of books. My comfy chair in the corner where I snuggle up and read with my very own light. It's my paradise! Invaders stay out! Except you. Lana, wait, don't go! I'm sorry. I didn't mean you. You're the best invader — I mean, friend. AHHH! I'm horrible to people sometimes. Oh gosh, did I hurt your feelings? I'm really glad you came over. Please stay.

MAKENA

(Talking to her friend, Erin.)

Erin, it's horrible! I feel personally responsible for the death of thousands of trees! All I did was join one nature organization. I wanted to save the animals. It only cost fifteen dollars and the wolf stuffed toy you got for joining was so cute. How could I resist? But now, I get big fat envelopes twice a week from every environmental organization on the planet. They all want me and they lure me in with these cute animal pictures on return address labels. I might fall for it if they'd spell my name right, but they usually don't. How could all these people who are supposed to care about the Earth waste all this paper on an eleven-year-old kid? Wait a minute. I got it. I'll write an article for the newspaper. "Stop the paper avalanche! Take kids off wildlife mailing lists." I'll mail it. Better idea! I'll e-mail it! Not another piece of paper will be sacrificed in this cause. Oh Erin, do you think it'll work?

YISHIA

(Talking to her friend, Avi.)

What would you do, Avi? It makes me crazy! Mom must be reading some kind of book about "how to encourage the intellectual growth of your middle schooler." She finds every chance she can to discuss some awful ethical situation. "What would you do, Yishia, if you had to chose between leaving your homeland and remaining loyal to your religion?" This she asks over breakfast! She used to ask, "So how's school?" *That* question was hard enough! But wait, she doesn't stop there. She states *her* opinion. Then she asks, "So what's yours?" Does she really want to know? Or does she just want me to agree with her? Avi . . . I don't have an opinion . . . yet. I can't answer questions like that. They're too hard. I haven't thought about all this yet. I'm not sure I want to.

ANGELINA

(Talking to her class.)

This is not stupid, OK? We were all supposed to choose something really important to us, and *this* is important to me. My research project will be . . . hey Paco, I heard that. You think I'm going to do something about sports. So what if I do? Just because your project is about the homeless you think it's better than mine. Yeah, well, six people in this class are doing the homeless! At least mine is original. My project . . . Timmy, the last time you laughed at me you paid for it on the playground, remember? Man, why does the teacher have to leave the room during my turn? Like you yahoos can stay focused?! She's always got something to "attend to." Well, right now, you're supposed to attend to me, so *listen up! (They do.)* That's more like it. My project — *(She checks for negative reaction. None.)* Better. OK . . . My research project is . . . wow. You guys are listening. You're really listening. My project is really important to *me*. "Why Women Should Make as Much Money as Men in Professional . . . Sports!"

CASSIE

(Talking to her mom.)

But Mom, look! The clay's starting to crack! Why?! I did everything Grandpa said: "Not too thick, not too thin." See?! The joints are falling apart, right where the legs of the horse bend. I had to make him running so his legs had to be bent. Oh no, a whole piece just fell off. Now he's ruined! Why does everything I make fall apart. I'll never be an artist. Stupid clay. *(She smashes a ball of the clay with her fist.)* Hey. This clay's still soft. Maybe I can patch it. Grandpa had a horse named Patches, didn't he? Yeah. That's who my statue can be. "Bumpy" Patches maybe, but still, it's better than giving up. Mom, why are you staring at me? Go on. Let the "artiste" work.

KIKO

(Talking to her friend, Ellie.)

You know why you're my best friend, Ellie? You understand me. Not like my stepmom. When Carol looks at me, her head kind of tilts, you know, cocks like a dog when it's trying to read your signals. And her lips draw up real tight like she's trying to smile, but she never does. She says, "I don't know what makes you tick." What does she think I am? A clock?! With a big round face all divided up into even little minutes ticking past? I'm more like a time bomb. Hey, that can be my new nickname: "Ka-blooy the time bomb!" *(Imitating a circus barker.)* "Come one, come all and see the kid who's about to burst into a million pieces! Why? Because her stepmom lights her fuse with all her nosey questions!" But you, Ellie. You always know how I'm feeling and just what to say to make me feel better. Ellie. What's that look on your face? It's blank. Like you don't get what I'm saying. Ellie, how could you?

DELIA

(Talking to her mom.)

It's a coupon book. I made it for you. You could redeem one of them today, Mom, if you want. They're for all kinds of things you like. This one's for "Delia's Shoulder Massage." I know you get tired being at your desk all day. My friends and I do really great massages. And this blue one's for two hours of car care. We could — *I* could wash your car. You could watch. I'll pull a beach chair out for you. We never use them anymore. Oh, this green coupon all decorated with words, it says, "Must be redeemed on a comfy couch or chair of your choosing." See, I read to you. Then you read to me. Could we do that one? Today? How long do you think you'll be on the computer, Mom? *(She waits for a reply.)* Mom? Happy Mother's Day.

YANG

(Talking to her grandmother.)

Try to understand, Grandmother. There is no mistake. This is money for us. Don't look so frightened. It is a lot, but Mother works hard so that you will have what you need and I can go to school. Please, give me the little paper. It's a check. I put it in the bank. Then we can take money and buy what we need. Oh, I wish I could make you understand. Hear my voice. It's happy! *(Speaking slowly, deliberately.)* " No more worry. Food. An apartment. Mother has a job." I should have kept going to those Chinese classes. "Grandma, you are here now. With us. No worries." You're smiling. Yes! Maybe you understand. Now give me the little piece of paper. Please? *(Grandmother gives the check back.)* Thank you, Grandmother. Xie Xie. See, I remember. Xie Xie.

> ** *Xie Xie, which means "thank you" in Chinese is pronounced "Shay-Shay."*

BENITA

(Talking to her mother.)

We need a code word, Mom. That's what our health teacher said. A code word or, better, a code *sentence* to use when you call your parents from a party, and you don't want to seem uncool, but you need to communicate that it is *way* time to come home. Mom! Think about it. When somebody pulls alcohol out of the fridge instead of Pepsi — *that* kind of code. I've got a couple of ideas. How about, "You're taking Dad where? To the emergency room?" No, Sabrina's mom works at the hospital. I'd get busted. How about this: "You got a kitten! I've *got* to come home right now!" Aw, Claudia would beg to come, too, and see I was lying. Wait. I got it: "Uncle Ernie *did* show up tonight by surprise?" Yeah, I can say Uncle Ernie is my long-lost relative that you're making me come see before he leaves at sunrise the next day. Perfect! OK. Let's practice. Mom. Have you been listening? This is a two-way street, if you want me to stay out of trouble. Isn't that what you want? So come on. Pretend the phone is ringing. Now say, "Hello." Hello?

INEZ

(Talking to her mother.)

Mira, Mommie. I got this from school for free. Flash cards. For you to learn English better. Watch. On one side there's a word. I say it, then you say it. Then you say the word that is opposite. Then we turn the card over and see if you were right. Let's try. *(INEZ holds up a card.) In.* "In." *Diga* "in." *(Mother is silent.)* Say "in." Then what about the opposite. *(INEZ acts it out.)* You come *in* the door, and when it's time to leave you go . . . Mommie, why won't you try? We'll still speak Spanish. In our house, on the street, in our family. But I want you to talk to my friends, my *new* friends. I want them to know *you. Por favor,* Mommie. *Para mi?* Let's see, what's on the next card. "Easy." Hard.

**Mira means "Look," *Diga* means "Say," *Por favor* means "Please," *Para mi* means "For me" in Spanish.

SALMA

(Talking to her older brother. Both are recent immigrants to the United States.)

I *was* watching him, Hamad. But he still got into trouble because none of the other little kids behave. Oh, their older brothers and sisters are standing around at the playground. But none of them watch like *I* do. No, they talk and joke and push each other on the swings, while their little brothers throw sand and their baby sisters cry! I need to be studying, Hamad. Just like you. Poppa didn't bring us to this country for me to be a babysitter! I am just as smart as you and I work just as hard. Stop laughing at me! In America, a girl can do anything a boy can do. *(Little brother is crying.)* Don't cry, Ali. Sister will get you a popsicle. And a Band-Aid. *(To HAMAD.)* I could be a doctor after fixing all these skinned knees. That's it! I'll go to medical school. You wait and see, Hamad. I can do *anything*.

FRANCES

(Talking to a group of girls at an audition for a play.)

So what's the problem, everybody? I came to this audition just like the rest of you. I've sung all the songs and played all the stupid little games. Now that it's callbacks — what *really* counts — why won't any of you be in my group? You scared of the competition? Fine. I'll be in my own group. Who needs any of you any way. Not me. I don't need anybody. *(Everyone in the group turns away from her.)* Go ahead. Turn your backs. Walk away. See if I care! No wait. Please. Somebody be with me. Please? I have to get a part in this play. Don't you get it? I have to . . . so I can be somebody else.

JORDON

(Talking to her cousin.)

Come on, Miranda. Quick. Before they call us in for supper.
This is the best time to jump on a trampoline, right before
a thunderstorm. The wind's blowing the trees and swirling
the clouds. Makes you dizzy as everything. It's great! Don't
worry about the lightning. The trees are higher than we
are, so if it strikes, it'll get them first. That's what Uncle
Kevin said. Why aren't you coming? Oh. Oh, I get it. You
don't want to play with me 'cause I'm the "little cousin."
You'd rather stay inside with the big teenagers who sit
around like slugs waiting for Grandma to serve the turkey.
You sure weren't like this *last* Thanksgiving! What's wrong
with you?! Why'd you have to go and turn thirteen?
Miranda. Please? Before the storm? *(MIRANDA doesn't
come.)* OK.

MARIA

(Talking to her dad.)

They're going to search my purse? In a museum?! I can't
open up my purse to that guy. I've got . . . stuff in there.
And all my earrings, they'll fall out if he turns it upside
down or shakes it or something. And my diary, what if he
reads my diary? And there's a three-day-old banana! He'll
be grossed out completely. You didn't tell me they'd search
my purse. This is crazy! Next they'll make us take off our
shoes like at the airport. I claim my constitutional rights
against unwarranted search and seizure! Dad. Let's just not
go in. Dad, honest. I'm *not* making up excuses. I'm totally
creeped out. I mean . . . I just came to see the paintings
and now I gotta think about bombs and crazy terrorist
and . . . Can just we go? Please?

KATIE

(Rene has just seen Katie copying a poem out of a book.)

Rene! What are you doing in here? Haven't you heard of knocking? No, don't say anything. Then you'll have to admit you were spying on me. Why wouldn't you spy on me? Who wouldn't want to see a great songwriter at work — to know how she comes up with all her wonderful lyrics that everybody loves — to learn her secret of how she always wins the school contests. Ha! I bet you're thinking that I use these poems and say I wrote them myself. Aren't you? Go ahead. Admit it! That's what you're thinking. Isn't it? Isn't it?! *(KATIE starts to cry.)* Please don't tell, Rene. How else can I keep winning? I have to win. That's what everybody expects from me. To be first. Always. I have to be perfect.

MICHELLE

(Talking to her friend, Ashley.)

Ashley, I told you! If you'd only listen to me I could save you so much heartache. But, no, you had to go steady with Derrick and now look at you. He's seeing somebody else and you are a miserable mess! *(Her cell phone rings.)* Hang on. My phone. *(She looks at the number.)* OMG, it's Derrick. Don't let him know you're here. Just use hand signals. Don't say a word! *(Answering the phone.)* Hello. Derrick, what a surprise. I thought you were out of town this weekend. Yeah. That's what you told Ashley. But I saw you at the mall with — *(ASHLEY is hand-signaling.)* -- uh, yeah the mall, uh, with — *(To ASHLEY.)* Why can't I say who with? *(To DERRICK.)* Uh, Derrick, how about *you* tell *me* who you were with! *(ASHLEY starts hand-signaling again wildly. To ASHLEY.)* Don't you want to make him confess? *(To DERRICK.)* What? Uh, I was talking to *you*, Derrick. *(To ASHLEY.)* What? Slow your hands down. *(To DERRICK.)* About that girl you were with — *(To ASHLEY, totally not getting her signals.)* Slow down! *(To DERRICK.)* So, Derrick. Derrick? You still there? *(He's not.)* You, my friend, must have flunked hand-signal school. Here, *you* call him back.

TELÉMACA

(Talking to a small child, Elena. They are both peasants in a small Mexican village.)

A turtle and a scorpion are beside a river. The scorpion says, "Carry me across the river on your back." "Certainly not," says the turtle, "You're a scorpion. You'll sting me." "No, I won't. Carry me across." So the turtle takes the scorpion on his back and starts swimming. Half way across the scorpion stings the turtle. "Why did you do that? Now we're both going to die!" The scorpion replies: "I can't help it. I'm a scorpion." Now do you understand, Elena? There will always be wicked people in the world, but we will not do what they ask. Now, we will go into the market together. We have a right to sell our corn and our flowers. No one can stop us, not even El Rico, the scorpion. Come. *(They see El Rico, an evil landowner.)* El Rico! Perhaps we should turn back . . . No. I am Telémaca. I am much, much wiser than the turtle. Come, Elena.

ARIADNE

(A small-time carnival entertainer, talking to LENNY on the dunes of east Texas in 1899.)

Aw, now Lenny. Anybody as smart and brave as you can fix a little ole flying machine. Why, you've got flying in your veins, flowing mighty as the Rio Grande, don't you now? Please, Sugar? Darling? *(LENNY doesn't answer.)* Oh, Lenny, don't make me put on my sweetie-pie carnival act. I'm done with all that silly chatter. I need you to listen to me. The *real* me. We've got the same dreams, you and me. I see it in you, sure as the sun rises each morning. You want to fly! To rise up in the air then look down and see all the people amazed, because they're watching a miracle. Your granddady made a miracle when he built that flying machine. But only you can fix it. Please, Lenny. Will you try? For me?

ATALANTA

(An Annie Oakley–like Wild West carnival gal, talking to a fella she just met.)

Ah, now, don't believe everything you hear, Lenny. I wasn't raised by no coyotes. It was bears! My real parents didn't want me 'cause I was a girl, so they left me out in the woods. Then a she-bear come along and found me. Raised me like one of her own. I was happy as a hound dog till the Queen of Wild West Carnivals up and adopted me. What's that face for? You don't believe me? Well, I'll show you one thing you can believe. I'm the surest shot in Texas. Step right on up here. Throw that ace of hearts in the air. I'll put three holes in it before it hits the dirt. Bam, bam, bam! *(Lenny keeps his dollar.)* It's just a dollar, Lenny. Could you just play along? My new momma will have my hide if I don't earn my keep before dinnertime. Help me out, would you?

CHAPTER TWO

Monologues for Young Men
(One minute or less)

TOSHI

(Talking to his friend at the beach.)

No, really. It's my best invention yet. See those pelicans?
When they dive for fish, first they spot them with one eye,
then blam! — into the waves. Score! Pelican lunch! But
these birds do it over — blam — and over — blam! — till
they go blind in their fishing eye. Then, know what they
do? They use their other eye — blam, blam, KABLAM! Till
they bust that one, too. Then they die! But I, enviro-men-
tal man, will single-handedly save the pelicans. By invent-
ing goggles for them! "Pe-goggles" or maybe "poggles." I
still have to decide on the name. See, we'll just put them
on all the pelicans . . . *(Discovering a major flaw in his
plan).* They'll know it's good for them . . . We'll just . . .
catch them . . . one at a time . . . *(Defeated.)* Aw, there it
goes. Another one of my best ideas SPLAT against the wall
of impossibility. "Poggles." How stupid is that.

ALAN

(Talking to his drama teacher.)

But I'm the prince! Hello! "Hamlet, *Prince* of Denmark?"
I've got to have a crown. Not a cheesy one, but a real one.
Claudius gets a crown and he's a lousy murderer. You gave
one to the Player King and Queen and they're *fake* royalty.
I'm the real thing! Watch. "Suit the action to the words,
the words to the action!" Wasn't that princely? *(Drama
teacher does not give.)* OK, I'm not always on time to
rehearsal. And Horatio and I messed around with the
swords, but we were practicing. Really! He wanted to see
what it was like to die since he's the only person in the
play who doesn't. We were "exploring the text" . . . like
you said! *(Teacher is still not giving in.)* The thing is . . .
see . . . I told my dad I'd be wearing a gold one, with jewels.
I had to tell him something . . . to get him to come. He's
never come. Now he'll think I'm a liar. And we'll fight. What
if I make it myself? Please?

PATRICK

(Talking to his dad.)

You don't believe me? I've got it all worked out. Football will make me rock in math! See, I'm gonna create an offensive philosophy toward algebra. I'll attack equations like a linebacker. I'll sprint through orders of operation with error-free execution. I'll pass "x" and "y" like a all-pro quarterback. I'll be a math machine! Destined for super-bowl grades! *(Realizing his dad's not buying it.)* Come on, Dad! I swear I'll get my grades up. Coach says they spend a bunch of practice just learning how to concentrate. That's got to help my grades. *Something's* got to help them. Let me be part of the team, Dad. OK?

DIMARCUS

(Standing with his cousin, Jamal, on a street corner.)

Taxi. Taxi! *(The taxi passes them by.)* Did you see that? He didn't have no fare. Back seat was as empty as anything. Now, watch this. He'll pull up big as you please, next corner. *(The taxi does.)* What'd I say! *(Calling out at the cab.)* Oh yeah, you pick up that lady and her briefcase, but pass me by like a comet! *(Cab can't hear him.)* He thinks I don't have the money to pay. Or I'm gonna rob him with the gun he's sure I got hid in my backpack. Oh yeah, I'm wild on drugs, too. Gonna hijack your cab! *(Cab drives off.)* Ignorant. Ignorant as that girl behind the counter at the 7-11. She jumped back three feet when I asked her the time. What, do I radiate danger? "Warning. Warning. Black teenager. Jump back. Beware!" It's sad, Jamal. Know what I mean? World ought to be past this. Guess our grandmomma was wrong. Still plenty of folks real quick to judge a book by its cover.

ENRIQUE

(Talking to his younger brother, Emilio.)

You just have to know how to play it. Like me, I say, "Poppy, it's just a party. No problemo." Then I smile real nice, tell him I'll be home whenever he says, then I go. He's too tired to stay awake till I get back, so it doesn't matter. Yeah, yeah, there's a curfew. But that's for sissies. If the police stop you, just act like you barely speak English and say, "Medicine for my sick mother." Then bolt like you're off to save her life and they leave you alone. Emilio, I'm your brother. It's my job to tell you how America works. Would I lie to you? *(Emilio is not sure.)* No. It is Poppy who lies. He said life here would be different. No more soldiers on the street to hassle you. No more war. No more fear. But what did we find? Police waiting like vultures for you to do something wrong. To throw you out of Poppy's "American Dream." Some dream. Poppy is still asleep, but me? I'm wide awake. You'd better wake up, too, little brother.

TERRELL

(Talking to his dad.)

What do you mean, Dad? The lady is gonna go wild for you. Look at you. New shirt. Been to the barber. Ain't nothing better lookin' ever gonna come that lady's way. She's no fool. Go on, find your car keys. You're making her wait. Ladies don't like to be kept waiting no matter how good-lookin' a man is. Take it from me. Yeah, I'm all over the lady thing. Trying to set an example for you. I ain't been sitting around all mope-y since Momma left. I been making my own way. You got to do the same. *(Dad is headed out the door.)* Hey Dad. You won't be out too late, will you? We're going fishing in the morning, remember? Don't forget. All right? Have fun, Dad.

RONNIE

(Talking to a friend, Melissa, while sitting on the swings.)

It was the weirdest thing. I had no idea how to answer. "Do you want to stay or go?" Danny said. Simple question. But it was like he'd asked me, "Do you want to discover a cure for cancer or build a colony on the moon." It felt like an earth-shattering decision. But we were just talking about "staying or going" at my house one afternoon after school Not *stay* on a deserted island or *go* to Antarctica. Just stay at my house or go to the movies. See, Melissa, they'd never asked me what I thought before. I didn't think they cared! So I couldn't say anything. *(He thinks for a moment.)* So . . . would you like to stay on the swings or go? I'd like . . . what *would* I like? I'm hopeless! *(Big pause.)* Let's stay. OK? I said it!

CARSON

Don't worry, Mom. I've got an easy Halloween costume.
The elephant god, Ganesh. Yuri gave me the idea in his
report on Indian gods. Ganesh is by far the coolest. I mean,
who wouldn't want to be the Lord of Success? The
Destroyer of all Evil! All I need is a trunk, some really big
ears, and a couple of extra arms. Oh yeah, a huge potbelly
would be good, too. Can I stuff pillows into Dad's gray
sweater? I'll just borrow it. And you've got sparkly beads I
can wear, right? Ganesh gets really duded out — ah, man!
What about the party? Cam will be such a pain if I show up
wearing beads. He's so stupid about girl stuff. Aw, Yuri will
really get it from Cam for wearing feathers. On his heels.
He's Hermes. Yuri learned about Hermes from me. Wish
Cam had learned something from mythology. Like how to
be cool! I'll have to think about the beads, Mom. We'll see.

MATT

(Talking to his dad.)

Lay off me, Dad! Sometimes you just have to swear! Like when you stub your toe really hard, or you drop your lunch tray, or when *you* are in the car and somebody cuts in front of you! Or is swearing one of those things grown-ups can do but kids can't?! What would *you* say if you really "messed" something up in a play-off game! But *fine*. I'll do your little exercise. You say swearing limits my vocabulary? OK, let's see. "You know that pass in the game, I really 'tanked' it." *(Dad gives him a look.)* You want better than that? OK. "I 'extremely missed' it." *(Dad gives him another look.)* More? "I 'failed to catch it.' I 'did not connect in a victorious way with the ball.'" Hey, that's a good one. How about: "I 'sacrificed the advantage of the team by my insufficient effort to retrieve the ball.' Or I 'valiantly leapt to block the hurling ball but, alas, to no avail!'" This is fun, Dad. Thanks!

EVAN

(Talking to a friend, Sarah.)

Who was Boo Radley, really? He's the spookiest character in the book, that's for sure. Hanging around in the shadows, creeping out Scout and Jim. Then these little treasures start to appear in a tree knot. Jim thinks they're from Boo, but Scout won't believe him 'cause Boo's this crazy creepy guy locked up in his basement down the street. Know what I think? I think it's the rest of the town that's crazy. Except Scout and Jim's dad, Atticus Finch. He's the hero of the book. But — oh, Sarah, how am I supposed to choose one character from a book like *To Kill a Mockingbird* to write about as my favorite? Why do teachers always ask you to do that? What does "favorite" mean? Most like somebody you know? Most like you? Who's gonna admit he's like Boo Radley — the guy nobody understands and everybody's mean to and afraid of. Who's gonna admit that? *(He thinks about that.)* Maybe me.

CHRISTOF

(Talking to his friend, Anton.)

So. Here's the new technique for studying. It's great! They taught us all about it in advisory. First you breathe deeply. *(He does.)* Then blo-o-o-o-w it out. Breathing keeps you calm. Relaxed. *(He does another big breath).* Blo-o-o-o-w. Now, I visualize myself taking the test, assigning a positive thought to each movement. I pull out my chair, I say "I will succeed." I sit down, I say "I am prepared." I lift my pencil, I say . . . I say . . . "Get me out of here! How's a kid supposed to know all this information after only six weeks of school? I couldn't *find* history class for the first week because all the halls look exactly alike! I couldn't use my book till last week because I forgot the combination to my locker. And now you want me to take a fifty-question multiple-choice test?" I visualize myself getting grounded till Christmas because I'm going to fail my first middle school exam. That is not a pretty picture. Man, I need a new technique. Anton, how do you study?

ADDISON

(Talking to his friend, Jason.)

If you've got to go, you've got to go, Jason! There's not a real bathroom for miles. This one's just . . . portable. Least it's not like the ones in Paris. I told you about them. First you have to figure out the right coin to use to pay to get in, then if you stay too long, which I did — don't ask. Too much ice cream on a boat ride. But these bathrooms are timed. They don't want the homeless people hanging out in them, so after four minutes, the door opens automatically, no matter what you're doing in there. So there I sat and sli-i-i-de, "Hello, Paris." Then this sprinkler goes off and almost drowns me to get me out of the port-a-potty *français*! Can you believe that? Don't laugh. Sure, it might be funny now. *(ADDISON starts to laugh, too.)* Yeah, it *is* funny now. Really funny! *(Imitating the sprinkler.)* Ka-bush! Whoa, Jason, don't laugh too hard. Quick, one's free now. Go!

ANDRE

(Talking to a new school friend.)

Say what? Outdoor recess? What's that? My old school, we came in the door when the bell rang and out the door at the end of the day. We were tough. See, they didn't want no kids running around outside. No place to run, 'cept the parking lot. We'd look out there from the windows on the third floor and see all kind of things going on. People hanging around, leaning on the cars. "No place for kids," that's what our teacher said. They said that for sure after a gun went off last April. For real! Yeah, we were tough. But here. Where'd you get all them trees and all that grass running way down that hill? Ball courts, too. They all for us? You sure? And . . . it's safe out there? *(The friend nods.)* Gimme that basketball. *(ANDRE runs outside.)*

MANUEL

(Talking to his mom.)

It's not fair, Mom. Everything bad Diego does is cute. Everything I do makes you blow like a volcano. Diego leaves his wet beach towel on the floor. You say, "Aw, doesn't he look cute flapping down the hall in my flip-flops." Diego leaves his toys all over the living room. You say, "Now let's play pirates and put all our treasure away." But when I leave my stuff, my property, in my *own* room on my *own* floor, you threaten to bring in a forklift and shovel everything out. "You're *older* now. You need to take more responsibility." Well, if anybody had told me this was the price of middle school, I would have stayed in fourth grade. Forever! *(Looks at his watch.)* We gotta go, Mom. Drive me to Caleb's house, then pick me up and take me to Josh's for soccer before the party that happens after the movie. What? I'm *older* now. You said. I got things to do.

BRYCE

(Talking to his school friend.)

So what's it going to be, Zach? Ancient Greece or Rome?
Come on! It's the most important part of our grade, so
we've got to pick something we can talk about *a lot.* Last
time we got stuck just trying to pronounce "Mesa . . .
Mesa . . . Mesopotamia." See, it still makes me nervous.
Why do we have to study all these ancient cultures anyway? Haven't we learned everything there is to learn about
long ago and far away? Like, look at this. *(He opens their
social studies book.)* "Pompeii." Who cares — Hey, get
this. Cool! *(Reading from the book.)* "The supposedly
dormant volcano above the town exploded in violent and
sudden eruption. Millions of tons of volcanic debris were
thrown up into a vast lethal cloud!" This is better than
TV! "The volcano was . . ." Oh no, how do we pronounce
Mount "Ve . . . ve-su-vi-oos?" Ah man, we are so are
doomed.

TREY

(Talking to a wild mustang, a horse he has been ordered by the court to help care for rather than serving time in a juvenile detention center.)

Look at you, wild mustang! Prancing all proud. Like me! Bet you fought out there in the wild, wild West. Yeah, I hear only one stallion can lead. Rest get driven out of the herd. So they go running round together causing trouble. Lazy, romping, fighting all day. Like me and my friends! Why'd you wanna come here after doing that? All locked up in a horse pen. Let's bust out, you and me! *(TREY steps toward the gate of the pen, but stops.)* They'd catch us. You . . . and me. Where'd we go? Nowhere *to* go. Ain't much land left for wild horses, that horse-trainer lady said. I asked her, "What's the world gonna do with the ones that are left?" She don't say. Maybe she don't know. What's gonna happen . . . to me?

JACK

(Talking to his little brother, Jed.)

Come on back up that beanstalk with me, Jed. First thing in the morning. All you gotta do is steer clear of the giant's wife. She'll pop you straight into the oven if she catches you. But we'll sneak past her, grab us something for our momma, then skitter right back down. I got us a hen last time. Lays the prettiest eggs you've ever seen. We would've starved, I tell you, if I hadn't got us that hen. Your belly's been full, ain't it? Well, you got *me* to thank. This time I'm gonna get me the giant's magic fiddle. It plays all by itself. Can't you see our momma if she had that fiddle? The smile would never leave her face. I'm gonna take it . . . uh, borrow it . . . just for a while. *(JED remains doubtful.)* Jed, that giant was fixin' to eat me for breakfast! It's all right to steal from somebody mean as him. Isn't it?

LENNY

(Talking to his friend.)

How do I know what a dream means? Don't know why I keep having it over and over. Grandpa is always standing out on a big open sand dune, holding a little kid's hand and a red balloon. They're both looking up at the sky or the clouds or . . . something. Grandpa has this big smile on his face, but then he stops smiling and reaches up fast and the red balloon floats away. I never see what the little kid does, 'cause I always wake up. He's probably just mad about losing the balloon. Aw, dreams don't mean anything! Except . . . Grandpa . . . he *does* look up, all the time, especially at the birds. Every time I catch him doing it, he looks away and tries to act like he wasn't looking anywhere. I do it, too. Like something inside me is dreaming when I'm awake. Dreaming of flying! But that's crazy! Isn't it?

SANDY

(Talking to his father.)

I am working so hard on this, Dad. So I can be an artist like you. It's a really complicated painting, with horizontals, verticals, diagonals. The diagonals are my favorite. *(He makes big diagonal strokes through the air.)* Swish! Swoosh! And I've got blue next to bright yellow next to *really* bright red. Red can be bright, right? Then there're the shapes. I want them to fly off the page, like swings on a trapeze! But this is a painting, not a trapeze. But I could build a trapeze, because I'm really an inventor! But . . . I *will* be an artist. Promise. *(Dad hands him a card.)* What's this? A card. From you? *(SANDY opens the card and reads it.)* "Dear Sandy. Not so many words. Art gives us something that words cannot." Wow. *(Smiling.)* That's all I'm gonna say.

GLASTON

(A young storybook hero is talking to his mother.)

You know the cave, Mother. It's the one above the field where I tend my sheep. The sheep never liked that cave. And when sheep don't like a thing, there's generally some reason for it. Well! *(Painting a very frightening picture with his story.)* Today, I heard faint noises coming from it, heavy sighs with grunts! So I took a look round the cave, slowly, quietly, then, Saints defend me, I saw him as plain as I see you! He's as big as four cart horses, all covered with slimy, shiny scales. And with every breath, fire flickered out of his nostrils! It's a dragon! *(Delighted.)* Isn't that wonderful?! I *knew* that cave must belong to a dragon. I'm not half as surprised as when you told me it *didn't* have a dragon. Oh, how I've longed to meet one — Mother? Did you just faint? I'm sure the dragon will be very nice. Oh dear.

CHAPTER THREE

Monologues for Young Women or Men

(One minute or less)

ALEX / ALEXIA

(Talking to a tutor.)

I can't open it. The math text book. I can't even reach toward it, or look at its shiny purple cover or thick black lettering or, worse, the squiggly white numbers that rise off the page like ghosts — laughing horrible ghosts! *(Tutor starts to leave.)* Wait! You don't have to get the counselor. I'm fine, Mrs. Preston. I just get a little dramatic. My uncle was an actor, so drama runs like a river through my veins. Did you see me in the school play? *(No reply.)* Right. Back to math. OK. Math. It paralyzes me, like a jellyfish or a giant fury tarantula or — there I go again! I should be on the Nature Channel. I get really carried away when I talk about animals. When I talk about anything . . . except math. It's all those numbers. How they turn into equations and quotients. It's like I'm trying to decipher hieroglyphics or a secret code! I . . . Mrs. Preston. I honestly don't . . . I wish I could describe it. It's a frustrating . . . awful feeling. When I open my book, I'm lost. Help me.

JORDAN / JORDANNA

(Talking to his/her dad.)

I can't eat that. I just got home from the dentist. She rearranged my teeth. I swear! Everything is in the wrong place. I don't remember her pulling anything. Hang on. I bet she put me to sleep and yanked out all my molars. It's a plot to get you and Mom to have to pay for braces for me! To trap you into spending thousands of dollars so the dentist's kid can go to college instead of me! I won't need to eat that broccoli or anything ever again if I'm not going to college. My life as I planned it is *over!* Dad, why are you still standing there with that plate of vegetables? Go away. *(Dad doesn't.)* OK. *One.* I'll eat *one.* Then can I have dessert?

CHRIS/ KRIS

(Talking to his/her dad.)

Dad, reading the newspaper *is* my homework. Promise.
That's one of the very cool things about seventh grade. The
teachers know we care about the bigger world. So they
encourage us to tune in and turn on to the news. OK, I
know I started with the sports pages. But there're some
very important national trends in there . . . areas of
national concern and . . . stuff. And I read the comics
because Mr. Whitman, my English teacher, says comics can
help you understand how stories work. You know, little
boxes of important moments. OK. Now I get to read the
front section. Yep. *(He/she hesitates.)* Gonna read the good
ole front page. *(He/she picks up the paper and silently
reads the headlines. She reacts to each one.)* Boring.
Boring. Interesting. *(He/she pauses over one.)* Scary. Can I
skip that one? Now see why I left this to read last?

TONY / TONI

(Talking to his/her dad.)

So, Dad. Here I am. Ready for my punishment. But you'll go easy on me, right? I just forgot to call home . . . again . . . when we left Nick's house. I know what I'm supposed to do. I just forgot. Dad, what's the matt knife for? Dad, please. Not that. Anything but that! You can hide the remote. Or lock the whole TV up in the garage. Just don't cut the plug off the cord like you did last time! I know I cheated the first three times you said no TV, but now you can trust me! I swear! *(Dad is starting to slice.)* Ahhh! Do you know how long it took Eddie to get that plug back on? He almost blew us all up. I'm not exaggerating. Please, Dad. Don't kill the TV!

TERRY/TERI

(Talking to his/her friend, Corey.)

Look at that. His feet are twitching. And watch his mouth. Even his whiskers move. He's dreaming. I know he is. He'll start whimpering soon, with little soft barks. Then his legs will start moving. Like he's chasing something. *(To the dog.)* What are you dreaming about, Scout? That white squirrel you saw in Granny's backyard? *(To his friend.)* You should have seen him. Scout saw that squirrel and turned into a pointer right before my eyes. *(To the dog.)* You dreaming about running around the park after your yellow ball? Huh? *(To his friend.)* Bet he's dreaming of his dog-lives past, when he hunted badgers for German royalty or herded sheep in Mongolia! I wish my dreams were as fun as his. My dreams aren't half this fun. When I'm asleep . . . or awake. What do you dream about, Corey?

AZIZ/ AZIZA

(Talking to his/her friend, Phuong.)

"Why can't I sit on this stoop? Kids should be outside — get fresh air. That is what they tell us at school. So here I sit. Breathing the air. There is plenty for you and me. I have as much right to the air as you." Do I sound American, Phuong? I want to. Oh, I wish I had said that to that man. He stood there with hate in his eyes. But I can say nothing. I have to be quiet. Respectful. Even when they look at me so afraid. "I am Arab, but an American, too," I want to say. "As American as you!" But he will never, ever feel that way, will he. How can we make this neighborhood understand me . . . you . . . all of us? Come on. Let's go outside . . . and breathe!

TYE / TIA

(Talking to his/her friend.)

Do you see that guy? He caught a baby shark and now he's got it lying on the beach. I *know* that's a baby shark. I know every fish in the *Sea Life Field Guide*. See? *(He/she references the book.)* "Atlantic Sharpnose Shark." Juvenile. They're endangered . . . I think. Doesn't matter. No fish should have to die on a beach with a bunch of people gawking at it. I'm going over there. I'll tell him to throw it back and now! *(He/she starts to go but stops.)* Like he's going to listen to me. I've tried this before. Remember the guy with the crabs? I said, "At least keep those crabs in water till you cook them!" He never even looked up from his crab pot. Like I was invisible. Bet this guy will look right through me, too, 'cause I'm a kid. *(Pause.)* Let's find out.

CARLOS / CARLA

(Talking to a friend, Rachel, at school.)

You want us to get a bad grade?! I thought we were partners on this project. Look, I took all these pictures, got them developed, bought the poster board, and printed out the map. What were you supposed to do? Just write three little index cards full of facts about the kind of rocks we found. That's all. It's due, tomorrow, Rachel! What did you do last night anyway? You promised you'd work on it when you went to your dad's. What happened? *(Rachel starts to cry.)* Rachel, hey. Hey, don't cry. Didn't you get to see your dad? You always see him on Thursday. Listen, don't worry about the rock facts. I'm all over it. OK? It's OK.

JAMAL / JAMILA

(Talking to his/her little sister in a drugstore.)

Wait for us outside, Daddy. We'll be right there. *(To his/her sister.)* You come here. You see that counter back there? You look long and hard. See all those folks sitting there drinking a coke and having a sandwich? All kind of folks, having themselves a fine Sunday afternoon? Don't you pull away from me! Now you picture our grandmother as a little girl. She couldn't anymore of sat down at that counter for a coke than you or I can fly to the moon this minute. But Daddy could when he was a kid. Because by then, this store welcomed folks at the counter no matter what color they were. Before anybody else around here did. Now here's you — you, with enough money in your pocket to buy that candy bar, thinking of sticking it in your pocket and walking out that door? Don't you ever, ever let me catch you doing that again. Grandmamma and Daddy didn't find their way through this world to wind up with somebody selfish as you carrying the family name. You hear me? You put that candy bar back or pay for it, one of the two. *(She puts it back.)* That's my sister.

KLAUS

(KLAUS is an apprentice to a Sorcerer. He/she is talking to an enchanted Cat.)

If the Sorcerer thinks I'm lazy, then lazy I will be! I'd much rather sit here all afternoon with my feet up, having a snooze, than clean up this old workshop. Why does it need to be clean anyway for the Sorcerer to do his magic? All he has to do is combine a little bit from this bottle, and a little bit from this jar, then read the magic spell from one of his books. *(KLAUS opens up one of the books.)* Let's see which spell he's got marked in the book to do today. Hey Cat, what's this? "How to reverse the flow of a river." Why would he want to do that? If the river flows away from the town, rather than toward it, the mills won't work and the boats will have to travel upstream to market and . . . You said he was a good Sorcerer! I've got to do something and quick. Me. Stop the Sorcerer? Me!

CHAPTER FOUR

Scenes for Two Actors

(3 – 6 minutes)

ALL GROWN-UP

CHARACTERS: (2 w)
  Chantal: 12 - 13
  Emma: 12 - 13

SETTING:
  In Emma's bedroom

EMMA and CHANTAL are good friends. EMMA's parents are divorced. CHANTAL has just arrived at EMMA's house, right after EMMA has come home from the mall. EMMA is pulling new clothes from a shopping bag.

EMMA: So which one should I wear? Don't you love the pink with the white skirt?

CHANTAL: Go for the denim skirt and that yellow top with the rhinestones!

EMMA: That's my favorite.

CHANTAL: Where'd you get all these great clothes?

EMMA: Where else? The mall.

CHANTAL: You win the lottery lately? How'd you pay for all this?

EMMA: I have to look spectacular! Dad's taking me to that restaurant near the water.

CHANTAL: Where all the beautiful people arrive in their boats!

EMMA: That's the one. It's really fancy.

CHANTAL: Then, girlfriend, *definitely* the rhinestones.

EMMA: I hope he likes it.

CHANTAL: My momma says all men like jewels, unless
    they have to pay for them!
EMMA: I love your mom.
CHANTAL: Then you can have her.
EMMA: Chantal! She's the best mom!
CHANTAL: I'm joking. So try it on.

*(EMMA pulls the yellow top on over a spaghetti-strap
shirt.)*

EMMA: I got earrings to match, too.
EMMA and CHANTAL: Rhinestones!
CHANTAL: Then we'll pick out your shoes. Your daddy
    won't know what hit him when he sees —

(The shirt is too big.)

EMMA: Oh no!
CHANTAL: Girl, you and me both could fit in that.
EMMA: It's not *that* big.
CHANTAL: But it's *too* big. And definitely *not* spectacular.
EMMA: I'll just wear the other one.
CHANTAL: You got earrings to match that one?
EMMA: No —
CHANTAL: Then say no more. Mom owes me a trip to the
    mall. We'll exchange it. I do it all the time.
EMMA: That's OK.

(CHANTAL starts to look through the shopping bag.)

CHANTAL: Where's the receipt?
EMMA: Receipt?
CHANTAL: Yeah.

EMMA: I didn't keep it.

CHANTAL: Didn't your momma teach you how to shop? Where's the price tag then?

EMMA: I —

CHANTAL: Sometimes they'll take it back just with that.

EMMA: I said I'll wear the pink one.

(CHANTAL finds a stack of price tags.)

CHANTAL: Here they are.

EMMA: Give me those —

(CHANTAL has seen the prices on the tags before EMMA gets them back from her.)

CHANTAL: Forty-nine dollars, sixty — How did you pay for these?

EMMA: I charged them.

CHANTAL: Emma —

EMMA: No, Mom gave me the money. She's got lots —

CHANTAL: No she doesn't.

EMMA: I just got them, OK?

CHANTAL: You didn't steal them —

EMMA: No —

CHANTAL: Did you?

EMMA: *(After a long pause.)* I had to.

CHANTAL: No you didn't. You can go to jail for that!

EMMA: Not if you don't get caught. Don't tell anybody, Chantal. Please! I *had* to take them.

CHANTAL: Why?

EMMA: I can't look like a kid.

CHANTAL: That's crazy.

EMMA: I'm *not* a kid. Because a kid would care that her dad is moving!

CHANTAL: He's what? When?

EMMA: Who cares! He can move if he wants. He left our family. He might as well leave town! A grown-up girl in rhinestones doesn't care. I don't — *(Starting to cry.)* — care!

(CHANTAL doesn't move at first, then she picks up one of EMMA's favorite stuffed animals and gives it to her.)

CHANTAL: Here.

EMMA: Thanks.

(EMMA takes the stuffed animal and cuddles it.)

EMMA: I'm *really* grown-up, huh.

CHANTAL: You gotta take this stuff back.

EMMA: I know.

CHANTAL: I'll go get your mom.

EMMA: No! Can we call yours?

CHANTAL: Sure.

(CHANTAL puts her arm around EMMA.)

CHANTAL: Sure.

End of Scene

PRIDE IN THE RIDE

CHARACTERS: (2 m)
    David: 12 - 13
    Lamar: 12 - 13

SETTING:
    David's room

> *DAVID and LAMAR are friends and classmates. DAVID is African-American. They have been given an assignment to make a short video about something in their community for social studies class.*

DAVID: All I know is that *I* am the on-camera personality!

LAMAR: Fine with me. *I* am the eye behind the lens. I see all and tell all.

DAVID: But what are we gonna tell? The video's due next week. We've got to decide.

LAMAR: I've decided.

DAVID: This is a team project, Lamar.

LAMAR: Then get on my team.

DAVID: Look, as long as I can say, "Good evening and welcome to our show" and a *whole* lot more, I'm cool. How about the museum? We could video all the old cars.

LAMAR: Nope.

DAVID: I thought you liked cars?

LAMAR: I like fixing them, not filming them.

DAVID: So what are we doing?

LAMAR: The number 22.

DAVID: Our bus?

LAMAR: That's right.

DAVID: What about our bus? It's just a bus! What can I say on-camera about a bus?

LAMAR: We'll start with you getting on at our stop.

DAVID: *(Picturing himself.)* I can see it. I talk, right?

LAMAR: Say whatever you want.

DAVID: "Here we are at our bus stop." *(Sarcastically.)* Oh yeah, that's thrilling!

LAMAR: Then we video *on* the bus.

DAVID: Is that legal?

LAMAR: Sure. Ought to be. We're capturing history.

DAVID: *(Doubtfully.)* We're taping a city bus!

LAMAR: That's history! Don't you get it? You know Mr. Johnson who gets on at 16th and Main?

DAVID: No.

LAMAR: He told my uncle he's ridden that bus every day for twenty years. And there's the lady who sits by the side door with her matching hat and purse.

DAVID: Remember her last Easter? Now *that* was a hat!

LAMAR: Has there been one Wednesday morning that she's not been on the 22? Where's she going?

DAVID: I don't know.

LAMAR: That's why we got to ask.

DAVID: Why's she gonna tell us? Two kids with a camera? We need something else, Lamar.

LAMAR: Where does everybody get on? Where're they getting off?

DAVID: Lots of places —

LAMAR: Know what I want to know more?

DAVID: You're gonna tell me.

LAMAR: Their stories! What they've seen and heard while taking that ride. You can interview everybody. I'll cut the camera back to you . . . a lot.

DAVID: *(Liking that idea.)* You will?

LAMAR: Ask them what they've seen —

DAVID: *(Imagining he's on camera.)* "What have you seen?"

LAMAR: And heard —

DAVID: "And heard and *felt* — "

LAMAR: Yeah, like that!

DAVID: "On the 22."

LAMAR: "Our little world on wheels."

DAVID: That's our title. I see it on the screen. *The World on Wheels.* Let's do it. Who do we start with?

LAMAR: Your great-granddaddy.

DAVID: Don't make me start with somebody half-deaf! He won't hear my questions!

LAMAR: How long has he been riding?

DAVID: I don't know.

LAMAR: Bet he didn't always ride in the front.

DAVID: He doesn't like to talk about those times.

LAMAR: Maybe he will now, if he knows you wanna listen. Maybe your great-granddaddy did a Rosa Parks. "I ain't moving to the back of this bus."

DAVID: *(A realization.)* Dang. History. Right on our 22 bus.

LAMAR: Let's sketch it all out. I'll make the storyboard of the shots. You write what you're gonna say.

DAVID: You should talk, too, Lamar. You got pride in our ride.

LAMAR: Now *that's* our title.

DAVID: Let's do it.

(The boys high-five each other.)

End of Scene

The Soccer Lesson

CHARACTERS: (2 w)
    Sita: 11 - 12
    Leanne: 11 - 12

SETTING:
    The basement of Sita's house.

SITA is a soccer star at her middle school. LEANNE has just moved to town and will be starting at SITA's middle school next week. SITA's mother invited LEANNE to come over. It was not SITA's idea.

SITA: So, what do you want to do?
LEANNE: I don't know. What do you want to do?
SITA: I don't know.

(Awkward pause.)

SITA: I hate this part. Figuring out what to do.
LEANNE: Yeah.
SITA: You like sports?
LEANNE: They're OK.
SITA: What PE did you sign up for?
LEANNE: Soccer.
SITA: Great. Let's play.
LEANNE: Inside?
SITA: We can pass.

(SITA gets her soccer ball.)

LEANNE: I don't know how.

SITA: What?

LEANNE: We didn't play soccer. At my old school.

SITA: Was your school on this planet?

LEANNE: We did other stuff.

SITA: Well everybody at our school plays.

LEANNE: Yeah. That's what I hear.

SITA: I'll show you how to push pass. Then when it stops raining, we can play in the alley. One-on-one.

LEANNE: That's OK. We don't have to.

(SITA starts to demonstrate.)

SITA: Plant your foot about hip distance from the ball. Imagine you've got a ball, then you can use this one. You've got to stand up.

(LEANNE gets up.)

SITA: Swing your other leg out and push the ball forward with the inside of your foot.

(LEANNE tries but wobbles.)

LEANNE: Whoa!

SITA: Steady!

LEANNE: How do you keep your balance?

SITA: Practice. It's fun. But don't hit too low or the ball goes airborne. And don't set too far away or you won't be able to control the ball. And make sure you point your plant foot at the target.

LEANNE: My plant foot?

SITA: The one not kicking!

LEANNE: Oh. I get it.

SITA: Offense passes the ball down the field, till someone — *(She mimes a big kick.)* Pow! Score!!

LEANNE: Gets it in the goal, right?

SITA: *(Running around as if celebrating a score.)* Go - o -
o - o - al!

LEANNE: I did play soccer once.

SITA: So you're not an alien. That's a relief!

LEANNE: I was in kindergarten. All I remember was this
big clump of kids running and kicking and the coach
telling me to get in there, too. "Kick, run!"

SITA: Did you?

LEANNE: And get kicked? No way. I wasn't a good runner.
I'm still not.

SITA: Then be goalie. The goalie is all by herself out on the
field.

LEANNE: That sounds good.

SITA: And you don't have to run the length of the field.

LEANNE: Even better.

SITA: And you get to use your hands.

LEANNE: *That's* the best.

SITA: You just have to block any shot that comes toward
the goal or the other team scores.

LEANNE: Oh. That's way too much responsibility.

SITA: You know, Leanne, you might want to take another
PE. There's tennis and track.

LEANNE: My mom says this is a soccer school. If I want to
fit in, I should play.

SITA: Yeah.

LEANNE: Who doesn't want to fit in? Thanks for the lesson, Sita. I should probably go.

(LEANNE starts to go.)

SITA: Hey. What *do* you like?

LEANNE: I don't know. Math. Art.

SITA: I'm pretty tight with the coach. I could ask if she needs help keeping our stats. You know, assists, saves, individual and team. If you want.

LEANNE: I could do that.

SITA: OK.

LEANNE: You guys need posters or anything? I could do that, too.

SITA: I'll introduce you to the coach.

LEANNE: I'll meet her . . . in PE.

SITA: You're gonna take soccer? Still?

LEANNE: Yeah.

SITA: You want to work on passing tomorrow, then?

LEANNE: Really?

SITA: Sure.

LEANNE: That'd be great. Sure. Thanks for having me over.

SITA: Thanks for coming. See you tomorrow. *And* at school.

LEANNE: That'll be good. *Really* good. Bye.

SITA: Bye.

(LEANNE exits. SITA dribbles the ball.)

End of Scene

ABUELA THE WISE

CHARACTERS: (1 w, 1 m)
 Juan: 10 - 12
 Nadia: 10 - 12

SETTING:
 Juan's room

> *JUAN and NADIA are cousins. Downstairs, there is a*
> *big family party to welcome their grandmother, who*
> *has been living with NADIA and her family, but who*
> *has just come to live with JUAN and his family. JUAN*
> *is imagining that he is up to bat in a baseball game.*
> *NADIA quietly opens the door and watches him. He*
> *does not know that she is there.*

JUAN: "Leading off first for the Panthers, Juan Arroyo. The
  pitcher fires. Crack! It's a long fly ball deep into center
  field."
NADIA: Did you make a home run?
JUAN: Don't you know how to knock?
NADIA: I never learned. Why are you hiding up here? The
  party's in the backyard.
JUAN: I'm busy.
NADIA: *Abuela* can't wait to see you play baseball.
JUAN: Yeah, well she might not get to! Stupid coach. He's
  always picking on me!
NADIA: *Todo el rato que está enojado, pierde de estar con-*
  tento.
JUAN: *(His Spanish is poor.)* What?

NADIA: "All time spent angry is time lost being happy."
    Abuela says that.
JUAN: *Abuela* isn't about to be kicked off her baseball
    team!
NADIA: No, but she's about to live with you and you won't
    even come down to welcome her.
JUAN: I said hello.
NADIA: Barely. You're lucky, you know.
JUAN: I don't feel lucky.
NADIA: She'll probably like you better than me, though.
    Mommie calls me a chatterbox. And *Abuela* always says
    "En boca cerrada no entran moscas."

(JUAN shrugs.)

NADIA: "Flies don't enter a closed mouth" and mine is
    always open.
JUAN: You can say that again.

(JUAN goes back to practicing his swing.)

NADIA: Don't you speak any Spanish?
JUAN: Some.
NADIA: *Abuela* will make you practice. She'll make you
    sing in Spanish and cook in Spanish —
JUAN: You know it wasn't my idea to have her come live
    here. That's all Mom's been thinking about, "Getting
    ready for Grandma." She should have been helping me
    with baseball!
NADIA: Aunt Gloria plays baseball?
JUAN: No — forget it.
NADIA: She said your coach wants you to go to a special
    clinic.

JUAN: Mom told you that?

NADIA: She told my poppy and I was listening. Why don't you go? It sounds fun.

JUAN: Fun if you've got a decent swing —

NADIA: That's why you should go. To get better.

JUAN: And have everybody on the team make fun of me? It's a clinic for babies. I'd be the oldest kid there.

NADIA: So?

JUAN: And I wouldn't know anybody.

NADIA: So?

JUAN: And what if it doesn't help. Huh? Maybe nothing can help.

(JUAN plops on his bed.)

NADIA: *El que no ariezga, no pasa el charco.*

JUAN: Would you stop?!

NADIA: "He who does not take a risk does not cross the puddle."

JUAN: What puddle?

NADIA: You're stuck. You have to jump. Jump into the puddle then out of it. *I* came up with the jumping part. A person gets wise having her grandmother around. You'll see.

JUAN: But . . . I can't talk to her, Nadia. And she's so old!

NADIA: *Hay que respectar las canas.*

JUAN: Translation, please.

NADIA: "One should respect gray hairs."

JUAN: Even *Abuela's?*

NADIA: Juan!

JUAN: OK, OK I'm joking.

NADIA: You better be. You better love *Abuela* or I'll take her back!

JUAN: It's just gonna be . . . different.
NADIA: There will be less puddles.
JUAN: You think?
NADIA: I know. I'm going to miss her. So much.
JUAN: So come visit.
NADIA: Can I?
JUAN: Sure. Whenever you want.
NADIA: I'll knock next time.
JUAN: Just come, OK?
NADIA: *Gracias*, Juan.
JUAN: So, is there still food downstairs?
NADIA: Plenty.
JUAN: I *am* hungry.
NADIA: So let's go.

(They begin to exit.)

NADIA: Why don't you show *Abuela* your swing?
JUAN: Yeah?
NADIA: I warn you, she'll have some pointers.
JUAN: *Bueno!*
NADIA: Listen to you! *Vamanos!*

(They exit.)

End of Scene

To help you with the language and culture in this scene:

Bueno: means "good."
Vamanos: means "Let's go."

El que no ariezga, no pasa el charco means
"He who does not take a risk does not cross the puddle."

Hay que respectar las canas means
"One should respect gray hair."

En boca cerrada no entran moscas means
"Flies don't enter a closed mouth."

Todo el rato que está enojado, pierde de estar contento
means
"All time spent angry is time lost being happy."

LADY LIBERTY

CHARACTERS: (2 w)
    Yasha: 11 - 12
    Alina: 9 - 10

SETTING:
    Near the rail of a steam ship pulling into New York
    Harbor, 1902.

*YASHA and her younger sister ALINA are at the end of
a long voyage across the Atlantic Ocean. They left
their home in Russia to immigrate to America. YASHA
is longing to see the Statue of Liberty in the harbor, but
ALINA refuses to budge from her spot on the inner
deck.*

YASHA: Alina, please. I know we can see her if we go just
    right over there. To the railing.
ALINA: No.
YASHA: Alina!
ALINA: I won't see her. My eyes are closed.
YASHA: Why, for heaven's sake? The beautiful lady in the
    harbor is waiting to welcome us.
ALINA: I don't want to see her.
YASHA: But Uncle Yuri, in his letters, he said she has a
    kind, warm face —
ALINA: She's a giant. I don't want to live in a country with
    giants.
YASHA: She's a statue!

ALINA: But she talks. Uncle Yuri said she talks. "Welcome," she said to him.

YASHA: With her face! Honestly, Alina. I promise, the Statue of Liberty does not talk. Come, we'll go see for ourselves.

(ALINA sits with greater determination.)

YASHA: Then . . . *(Trying another tactic.)* Why don't we go see what birds are in the harbor.

ALINA: I don't like birds.

YASHA: Yes you do.

ALINA: I've had them flying all around me for weeks. Why didn't you shoo them off?

YASHA: I tried. They were looking for food. They're just as hungry as we are.

ALINA: My stomach hurts.

YASHA: Well . . . there is food waiting for us.

ALINA: There is?

YASHA: In America. Come to the railing and see. As soon as we get off the ship, they'll ask our names and who we will live with.

ALINA: Then we'll see Uncle Yuri?

YASHA: He'll be waiting on the dock in "New York City." How I love saying those words.

ALINA: I don't. The streets are filled with carriages that go so fast they squash you and buildings so tall they hide the clouds and no apples!

YASHA: No apples?

ALINA: The old man sitting right over there said. No apples at all.

YASHA: But the streets are made of gold. Come see.

ALINA: That's a dream. The old man said.

YASHA: But they are *like* gold. They must be. Please, Alina, come to the railing with me.

ALINA: No.

YASHA: Then I will go alone.

ALINA: You can't!

YASHA: I will!

(YASHA starts to cross away from ALINA.)

ALINA: Yasha, no! You promised Papa.

YASHA: *(Repeating her father's words.)* "Never to let you out of my sight."

ALINA: So you can't go.

(YASHA slowly sits next to ALINA.)

ALINA: When can we go home, Yasha?

YASHA: We are home.

ALINA: Here?

YASHA: Yes.

ALINA: We're never going back?

YASHA: No.

ALINA: Ever?

YASHA: Papa will join us here.

ALINA: When? When, Yasha?

YASHA: *(She doesn't know.)* Soon. Very soon.

(They sit silently for a moment.)

YASHA: She holds a light like an angel, Alina. I've seen her in my dreams. "Lady Liberty."

ALINA: The giant?

YASHA: The *angel*.

ALINA: With wings?

YASHA: I'm not sure.

ALINA: I'd like her if she had wings.

YASHA: Oh . . . well, she *might* have wings.

ALINA: Will you hold my hand?

YASHA: Always.

(The sisters stand and step to the railing together.)

End of Scene

GLOBAL-WARMING MONSTER

CHARACTERS: (2 w)
  Andrea: 11 - 12
  Mina: 11 - 12

SETTING:
  Their classroom

> *ANDREA and MINA are partners on an end-of-the-year*
> *science project. Their topic is global warming. It is*
> *two hours before they are to present their project to*
> *their classmates, teachers, and parents.*

ANDREA: Have you got all the index cards?

MINA: I think so.

ANDREA: We are going to *rock* in this presentation.

MINA: Yeah.

ANDREA: Nobody has the stuff we do — the maps, the model of the Earth all wrapped in a blanket.

MINA: Do you think they'll get what's happening with the carbon dioxide?

ANDREA: I made the arrows bigger last night on my computer. And labeled them with big yellow letters — "CO^2 trapped and returning to earth." Then I put a big headline —"The Earth is Being Eaten by the Global-Warming Monster."

MINA: That should get their attention.

ANDREA: I want the whole world's attention. Don't you?

MINA: Of course.

ANDREA: So you're going to present our model of the ice caps melting, right?

MINA: No, you. I get too sad about the polar bears.

ANDREA: Then you do coral reefs. How they're turning white. Dying from lack of nourishment. The end of the underwater paradise! Man, I wish we had some really scary music to play.

MINA: You do coral reefs, too. You make it all sound really bad, which is good.

ANDREA: Then, what will you do?

MINA: You . . . can do *all* the presentation part. I did a lot of the research, so that should get me a decent grade.

ANDREA: Mina, what are you talking about? We've been working together on this for weeks. Our parents are coming to see us do it!

MINA: Exactly.

ANDREA: Exactly what?

MINA: My mom is coming. So I need to sit it out. You'll do great.

ANDREA: I need a map, here, Mina. I'm lost!

MINA: She got a new job.

ANDREA: Congratulations. So?

MINA: She's working for the government now. It's some department that deals with lots of regulations and things.

ANDREA: So?! OK, you do droughts and hurricanes —

MINA: I can't!

ANDREA: Why?!!

MINA: Cause my mom's new boss makes laws — rules about the environment. And he doesn't believe in global warming.

ANDREA: Where does he live? In a cave?!

MINA: He'll be at the presentations! He's Jared's dad in eighth grade. Mom's his secretary.

ANDREA: Oh.

MINA: What if what I say makes him mad at her?

ANDREA: It won't.

MINA: It could! It took Mom a long time to get this job. What if I mess it up for her?

ANDREA: *(Very disappointed.)* But we were going to save the world.

MINA: We will. Just maybe not this afternoon.

ANDREA: I thought this mattered to you, Mina!

MINA: It does.

ANDREA: Incredible. Unbelievable. What's more important? Your mom's job or the world?

MINA: How can I answer a question like that? What's the meaning of life, Andrea? Answer that one!

ANDREA: Life won't have any meaning if there isn't any.

MINA: Any what?

ANDREA: Life! If it's all gone by the time we grow up.

MINA: It won't be.

ANDREA: It might. I don't want to live in a melted-down world. Do you?

(MINA doesn't answer.)

ANDREA: OK fine. I'll do the whole thing myself.

(ANDREA starts to leave the classroom.)

MINA: Don't leave out the last part. About what everybody can do to stop it.

ANDREA: Fine.

MINA: That's the most important part!

ANDREA: Yeah. It was *your* part. You wrote that whole part!

(ANDREA is almost out the classroom door.)

MINA: Wait!

(ANDREA stops.)

MINA: I'll do that part.
ANDREA: You will?
MINA: Maybe the eight graders will go first and Mom's boss will leave.
ANDREA: Or you can wear a disguise!
MINA: *(Laughing.)* Andrea.
ANDREA: I've got some of those glasses with a mustache.
MINA: That's OK!
ANDREA: Don't say I didn't offer. Mina, your mom will be proud of you. You're standing up for what you believe in. She gave you that Shakespeare T-shirt you wear all the time, didn't she? It says "To thine own self be true."
MINA: I should have worn it today.
ANDREA: Come on, let's get everything set up.
MINA: I'm there. Let's go.

(ANDREA and MINA exit the classroom.)

End of Scene

OVER THE RAINBOW

Adapted from *Broken Rainbows*

CHARACTERS: (1 w, 1 m)
  Joel: 13 - 14
  Gina: 13 - 14

SETTING:
  The steps of Joel and Gina's apartment building on a
  hot summer night.

  GINA and JOEL live in an inner-city apartment com-
  plex. GINA, African-American, has lived here all her
  life. JOEL, Jewish and from a middle-class neighbor-
  hood, has recently moved here after his parents'
  divorce. As the scene begins, GINA comes out of the
  front door of the apartment building. She is drinking a
  soda. At the same moment, JOEL comes storming out,
  fresh from an argument with his mother.

GINA: *(Calling back to her apartment on the third floor.)*
  I'll be back up in a minute. It's too hot up there. I'm
  just gonna sit on the steps — *(Enter JOEL.)* Hey, Joel,
  slow down. Why you hurrying on a night like this? All I
  wanna do is cool down.
JOEL: *(Pacing.)* Me, too.
GINA: *(Realizing there is something wrong.)* There's a
  breeze here if you wanna sit.
JOEL: I wanna explode!
GINA: It's too hot for that. Come on. Sit. *(JOEL finally*

crosses to the steps and sits.) We got so many fans goin' upstairs, sounds like a church choir, all hummin' at different pitches. You got an air conditioner?

JOEL: No! Can't afford it . . . *now.*

GINA: We're supposed to get one next week. My momma, she's crazy. Bought a rug before she bought an air conditioner, in summer! But she had her heart set on this braided rug, and mommas deserve to get what they want.

JOEL: Yeah, well sometimes they can't get it.

(JOEL stands up to go.)

GINA: So how's it working at the community center? You do recycling, right?

JOEL: Gets pretty old pretty fast.

GINA: But it's important.

JOEL: You don't have to tell me.

GINA: Then you tell me.

JOEL: Around here, I get called "Munchkin." But at my old school, I was "the enviro-maniac!"

GINA: *(Laughing.)* What?

JOEL: I got my whole school to recycle everything. I organized my old neighborhood to share their newspapers. I get pretty crazy about it. I just wanna make a difference, y'know?

GINA: My momma says if you wanna change the way things are, start with yourself. Then it'll ripple out. Change other people. So I shouldn't toss this soda can in any-ole dumpster around you, huh? *(They share a laugh. JOEL sits.)* If *I* were cleaning up the planet, I'd do a lot more than pick up the garbage. I'd turn the whole world into the Land of Oz — an Emerald City.

JOEL: *(Laughs.)* Over the rainbow, right?

GINA: You think it's that far?

JOEL: I'd make a world where dads don't get married six months after they dump your mom.

GINA: Hey, I'm sorry.

JOEL: Yeah. I gotta go. Mom wants Chinese food.

GINA: Plenty of that in this block. You starting to feel at home around here?

JOEL: Honest answer?

GINA: Better be if we're gonna be friends.

JOEL: I don't know where home is anymore.

GINA: Just like Dorothy.

JOEL: What?

GINA: In *The Wizard of Oz?* You know . . .

JOEL: Right. Over the rainbow. See you around.

GINA: How about tomorrow right here? Ain't gonna be any cooler anytime soon. Inside or out. *(She means the weather and JOEL.)*

JOEL: You got that right. Thanks, Gina. I'll see you tomorrow.

GINA: Promise?

JOEL: Would a munchkin lie?

GINA: You tell me.

JOEL: *(Honestly.)* Right here. Tomorrow.

(JOEL exits. GINA smiles and watches him go.)

End of Scene

PLAYING TO BE HEARD

Adapted from *Broken Rainbows*

CHARACTERS: (1 w, 1 m)
    Gina: 13
    Damond: 14

SETTING:
    The lobby of the auditorium of a middle school.

GINA, an aspiring musician, is folding programs in the lobby of the auditorium of her school in preparation for an upcoming musical. Her friend JOEL is in the musical. JOEL also works with DAMOND at the community center. DAMOND, GINA's brother, comes in with his saxophone. He plays a loud riff.

DAMOND: Aww, put me in a television commercial.
GINA: Don't play that in here. They're practicing onstage. They can hear you!
DAMOND: My sax is my voice, my choice, my means of communication.

(He plays another riff.)

GINA: Go communicate outside before you get me in trouble. Ms. Beech needs me to fold every one of these programs by four o'clock. Leave me alone.
DAMOND: Thought you'd like a serenade while you slave for the music-theater god.

(As DAMOND turns to leave, GINA sees a can of spray paint in his back pocket.)

GINA: Damond! What's that in your pocket? Spray paint?!

DAMOND: I've been communicating visually, too.

GINA: If you are tagging for some gang —

DAMOND: I am expressing myself. I keep a stash in the trash on the court, so when the urge strikes to speak, I streak. Artist of the street. *(Plays a loud riff on his sax.)*

GINA: Shhh!

DAMOND: What, you afraid your new boyfriend's gonna be disturbed in his almighty rehearsal?

GINA: At least Joel's got dreams. What have you got? Spray paint!

DAMOND: You listen, sister. That Joel is loser-material. Like every one of them new boys who comes moving into this neighborhood, thinks he's gonna be king of the hill — top o' the heap.

GINA: And what are you doing to get off the bottom?

DAMOND: You think I don't have it together?

GINA: You call spray painting "together"?

DAMOND: "Recreation," Gina. I'm "re-creating" the world the way I see it. I *ain't* on the bottom no more, so why should I keep quiet?

GINA: You'd better keep quiet with that spray paint around Momma. She'd run you out if she knew.

DAMOND: Yeah? What if she knew I was the Worker of the Week at the Community Center? Not just this week, but last week, too?

GINA: Why didn't you tell us?

DAMOND: Why didn't you ask? No, you're too wrapped up in your little dreamworld. You and Joel on Broadway or

Hollywood! Doesn't matter to you *what* I do, as long as you get what you want.

GINA: What I'm gettin' now is hurt.

DAMOND: Yeah, well welcome to the club!

(They stare at each other, angry, hurt.)

DAMOND: *(Trying to turn things around.)* Gina. Let's get on out of here —

GINA: I've got to finish these programs.

DAMOND: Sure. Sorry to take your time. You get on back to your job. Be a good little girl, now. That's right —

GINA: That's right!

(DAMOND turns to go.)

GINA: Damond, wait . . . Momma's getting off early tonight. When I'm done, let's all have some supper —

(DAMOND walks out.)

GINA: Damond!

(DAMOND is gone. GINA starts to fold the programs, but then she stops.)

End of Scene

THE QUEST

Adapted from *Perseus Bayou*

CHARACTERS: (1 w, 1 m)
   Andy: A sword-swooping gal
   Percy: A would-be hero on a quest

SETTING:
   An island in the bayou of Louisiana

Perseus Bayou resets the Greek myth of Perseus and the Medusa in the Louisiana Bayou right after the Civil War. In this scene, ANDY [Andromeda] is a wild can-do gal who dreams of adventure. PERCY [Perseus] is a boy whose pride has gotten him into a dangerous quest. He must find the snake-headed monster, the Medusa, who lives deep in the swamp. PERCY has just arrived on ANDY's island. ANDY pounces on the unsuspecting PERCY.

ANDY: A-YIYIYIYIYIYIYI!

(ANDY steals PERCY's sword and wrestles him to the ground, pinning him.)

ANDY: How dare you trespass on my land!
PERCY: Give me back that sword. It's mine!
ANDY: Surrender now, intruder!
PERCY: I didn't do anything.
ANDY: Then give. You give?

HE QUEST

ed from *Perseus Bayou*

ACTERS: (1 w, 1 m)
dy: A sword-swooping gal
rcy: A would-be hero on a quest

NG:
island in the bayou of Louisiana

seus Bayou *resets the Greek myth of Perseus and
Medusa in the Louisiana Bayou right after the
l War. In this scene, ANDY [Andromeda] is a wild
do gal who dreams of adventure. PERCY
seus] is a boy whose pride has gotten him into a
gerous quest. He must find the snake-headed mon-
the Medusa, who lives deep in the swamp. PERCY
ust arrived on ANDY's island. ANDY pounces on
nsuspecting PERCY.*

YIYIYIYIYIYIYI!

Y steals PERCY's sword and wrestles him to the
d, pinning him.)

w dare you trespass on my land!
ive me back that sword. It's mine!
rrender now, intruder!
didn't do anything.
en give. You give?

PLAYING TO BE HEARD

Adapted from *Broken Rainbows*

CHARACTERS: (1 w, 1 m)
   Gina: 13
   Damond: 14

SETTING:
   The lobby of the auditorium of a middle school.

   *GINA, an aspiring musician, is folding programs in
   the lobby of the auditorium of her school in preparation for an upcoming musical. Her friend JOEL is in
   the musical. JOEL also works with DAMOND at the
   community center. DAMOND, GINA's brother, comes in
   with his saxophone. He plays a loud riff.*

DAMOND: Aww, put me in a television commercial.
GINA: Don't play that in here. They're practicing onstage.
   They can hear you!
DAMOND: My sax is my voice, my choice, my means of
   communication.

   (He plays another riff.)

GINA: Go communicate outside before you get me in trouble. Ms. Beech needs me to fold every one of these programs by four o'clock. Leave me alone.
DAMOND: Thought you'd like a serenade while you slave
   for the music-theater god.

(As DAMOND turns to leave, GINA sees a can of spray paint in his back pocket.)

GINA: Damond! What's that in your pocket? Spray paint?!
DAMOND: I've been communicating visually, too.
GINA: If you are tagging for some gang —
DAMOND: I am expressing myself. I keep a stash in the trash on the court, so when the urge strikes to speak, I streak. Artist of the street. *(Plays a loud riff on his sax.)*
GINA: Shhh!
DAMOND: What, you afraid your new boyfriend's gonna be disturbed in his almighty rehearsal?
GINA: At least Joel's got dreams. What have you got? Spray paint!
DAMOND: You listen, sister. That Joel is loser-material. Like every one of them new boys who comes moving into this neighborhood, thinks he's gonna be king of the hill — top o' the heap.
GINA: And what are you doing to get off the bottom?
DAMOND: You think I don't have it together?
GINA: You call spray painting "together"?
DAMOND: "Recreation," Gina. I'm "re-creating" the world the way I see it. I *ain't* on the bottom no more, so why should I keep quiet?
GINA: You'd better keep quiet with that spray paint around Momma. She'd run you out if she knew.
DAMOND: Yeah? What if she knew I was the Worker of the Week at the Community Center? Not just this week, but last week, too?
GINA: Why didn't you tell us?
DAMOND: Why didn't you ask? No, you're too wrapped up in your little dreamworld. You and Joel on Broadway or

Hollywood! Doesn't matter to you *wha̶*
you get what you want.
GINA: What I'm gettin' now is hurt.
DAMOND: Yeah, well welcome to the club

(They stare at each other, angry, hur̶

DAMOND: *(Trying to turn things aroun̶*
on out of here —
GINA: I've got to finish these programs.
DAMOND: Sure. Sorry to take your tim̶
to your job. Be a good little girl, no̶
GINA: That's right!

(DAMOND turns to go.)

GINA: Damond, wait . . . Momma's ge̶
When I'm done, let's all have som̶

(DAMOND walks out.)

GINA: Damond!

*(DAMOND is gone. GINA starts̶
but then she stops.)*

End of Sce̶

PERCY: *(Pinned.)* Yeah.
ANDY: Say "I give."
PERCY: I give! I give!
ANDY: Woo-hoo!

(ANDY jumps around victoriously, pulling the scarf off her head. Her long hair is revealed.)

PERCY: What the — What's a girl doing out here in the swamp?
ANDY: I can be anywhere I want. My daddy's the mayor of this whole island.
PERCY: Why are you all dressed up like a boy?
ANDY: Why shouldn't I be?
PERCY: 'Cause you're so . . . *(She is.)* pretty.
ANDY: You sound like my momma. "Andromeda, you're the best-lookin' girl in Louisiana."
PERCY: *(Dreamily.)* "Andromeda . . . "
ANDY: *(Threatening PERCY with her fist.)* Don't call me that. It's Andy, all right? My momma lines up one silly boy after another to come courting me. I don't want a boy! I want adventure!
PERCY: I'm on an adventure, Androme — *(Catching himself.)* Andy. See, a panther named Hermes gave me this sword. And now I'm looking for the land of the gray ghost sisters so I can find my way to the snake-headed Medusa.
ANDY: *(In awe.)* Can I be you?
PERCY: *(Boasting.)* Then I've got to cut off her head.
ANDY: Why?
PERCY: 'Cause I promised I'd bring it back to the evil Polydectes.
ANDY: You told him you could kill the snake lady?

PERCY: (Ashamed.) I told him I could do anything.

ANDY: Don't you go making boasts like that around here. Our parish is haunted by some kind of evil creatures. They don't like it when us human folks start to bragging. They live out in the swamp.

PERCY: (Afraid.) This swamp?

ANDY: You'll hear them. Growling in the night. Then your dog will disappear right off your porch. Or your whole catch of fish — (Snapping her fingers.) gone in the blink of an eye.

PERCY: They out here now?

ANDY: Will be, if you keep bragging like a proud peacock! Ever since my momma's been boasting about my being so pretty, three dogs — (Making a gobbling-up gesture and sound.) Gone! But I'm not scared, no matter what that greedy monster is.

PERCY: That makes one of us.

ANDY: Let me come with you, Percy. We'll slay that Medusa for good and all.

(ANDY does some impressive sword moves, imagining she's fighting the Medusa.)

PERCY: But Andy, wait! You can't look at her. If you do, you turn to stone.

ANDY: Oh. Then we won't look! En garde.

(ANDY swoops her sword. PERCY tries to duplicate her move, but he is a real beginner.)

ANDY: That's it!
PERCY: AHHH!

(PERCY spins around like a top and falls.)

ANDY: Sort of. Tell you what . . . what's your name?

PERCY: Percy. Perseus Bayou.

ANDY: I'll make you a pouch, Percy. You got to have something to put the Medusa's bloody head in.

PERCY: I hadn't thought of that.

ANDY: You go see those gray ghost sisters, then meet me right where the bayou curls like a snake to the south. You got that?

PERCY: Where the bayou curls like a snake to the south.

(ANDY starts to go.)

ANDY: Hey Percy. *(PERCY turns back immediately.)* Good luck.

PERCY: Thanks.

End of Scene

LYING SPIRIT CAT!

Adapted from *Perseus Bayou*

CHARACTERS: (1 w, *1 w or m)
    Andy: A sword-swooping gal
    *Hermes: A spirit cat, timeless

SETTING:
    Where the bayou curls like a snake to the south, 1870

    Perseus Bayou *resets the Greek myth of Perseus and
    the Medusa in the Louisiana Bayou right after the
    Civil War. In this scene, ANDY [Andromeda] has just
    arrived at the place where PERCY [Perseus] promised
    to meet her. But she finds HERMES, a magical panther,
    waiting for her instead.*

ANDY: Percy! I made you a pouch like I promised. For the
    Medusa's bloody head! Where are you?
HERMES: *(Hiding in the shadows.)* Little girls shouldn't be
    out in the swamp at night.
ANDY: *(Pulling her sword.)* Who's there?
HERMES: Loup-garoux, a werewolf, is waiting to get you.
ANDY: I don't believe in loup-garoux. *(To herself.)* Not
    much anyway. *(To the voice.)* You such a coward you've
    gotta hide? Come out and fight.
HERMES: As you wish. Gerrrrrr!

    (HERMES leaps out and tries to pounce on ANDY. But

ANDY through rapid, impressive sword moves pins HERMES.)

HERMES: Ahhhh!

ANDY: I don't like critters much, especially when they talk. I'll give you five seconds to make a new trail outta this bayou and don't you ever come back.

HERMES: All right. But if you're looking for Percy, I know where he is.

ANDY: Where?

HERMES: Let me up and I'll tell you.

(HERMES starts to stand up, but ANDY grabs him by the ear.)

HERMES: Ye-ouch!

ANDY: You listen here, spirit cat. Percy needs my help fighting a snake-headed monster, so if you know where he is, you tell me quick.

(ANDY lets go of HERMES.)

HERMES: He doesn't need your help, 'cause he's gone. He turned tail like a scared little puppy.

ANDY: He did? I don't believe you.

HERMES: Before he ran off home, he told me he'd met some funny-dressed girl in the swamp, but he didn't care one bit about ever seein' her again.

ANDY: He said that?

HERMES: Guess he's not the hero-boy you thought he was.

ANDY: But he promised to meet me right here!

HERMES: I don't see him here. Do you? Here, chick, chick,

chick, chick, chicken! Better run before your momma comes looking for you. Callin' her baby girl home!

ANDY: You're a lying spirit cat. I'm gonna find me the truth and Percy . . . somehow.

(ANDY runs off, intently.)

HERMES: *(Laughing to him/herself.)* Good luck.

End of Scene

TIGER IN A TRAP

Adapted from *Dancing Solo*

CHARACTERS: (1 w, 1 m)
    Kara: 13 - 14
    Jake: 13 - 14

SETTING:
    In front of school by the pay phones.

KARA and JAKE have been going together for a few months. But lately, JAKE's behavior has become very odd. He is distant, distracted. KARA, who is insecure, is afraid of losing her boyfriend, but even more afraid of what might be wrong. KARA does not know that JAKE has become involved with drugs. KARA has just come looking for JAKE.

KARA: Jake! Where've you been? I've been waiting for you in the library.

JAKE: I gotta stay out here.

KARA: By the pay phones? *(Trying to joke.)* Are you expecting a call from one of your other girlfriends?

JAKE: I don't think that's funny.

KARA: I was just teasing. Why didn't you meet me after lunch?

JAKE: I was . . . busy.

KARA: I saw you out in the parking lot.

JAKE: No you didn't.

KARA: Yes I did. Who was that guy in the car you were

talking to? You're not supposed to be out of the building —
JAKE: I wasn't out there, OK?!

(JAKE breaks away from her.)

KARA: OK. *(JAKE paces.)* What's going on? You look like
you're doing a tiger imitation.
JAKE: I'm just . . . hanging out.
KARA: But you're all —
JAKE: *Lay off*, Kara.
KARA: Sure . . . So. Wanna hear something great? I've got
this great idea. Don't you want to hear it? My outra-
geously romantic idea for after the dance?
JAKE: Whatever. Sure.
KARA: We're still going, aren't we, to the dance?
JAKE: *(Pacing, distracted.)* What? Oh yeah, sure.
KARA: Well, Dorien's uncle has this boat, and he and
Melody are going out on it after the dance. Cruising up
and down the river. Isn't that a beautiful image — just
two people and a boat?
JAKE: I don't have a boat. Sorry. OK?
KARA: Jake —

(The pay phone rings.)

KARA: That's weird. I'll answer it.
JAKE: *(Crossing in front of her.)* No.

*(He picks up the receiver, listens quickly, then hangs it
up again.)*

KARA: What're you doing? Why are you acting like this?

JAKE: Kara, listen. I've got to go to class in a minute.

KARA: I know. *(Trying to change his mood.)* And you still haven't said one sweet thing to me.

JAKE: I need your help.

KARA: Anything.

JAKE: If the phone rings again, I want you to pick it up, then just hang up again.

KARA: Why? Is it for you?

JAKE: Just *do* it. Please. *(He touches her on the cheek.)* You're great, Kara.

(JAKE exits.)

KARA: Jake. What's going on? Why won't you tell me?!

(The phone rings. KARA lets it ring a second time. She picks it up and listens for a moment, then speaks.)

KARA: Who is this? Who *is* this? Are you calling for Jake?

(The party on the other end hangs up. KARA stares at the phone.)

End of Scene

WHAT DO YOU KNOW, PINOCCHIO

Adapted from *Mississippi Pinocchio*

CHARACTERS: (1 m, *1 w or m)
  Pinocchio: A wooden puppet, who has recently come to life
  *Cricket: An ancient and wise creature

SETTING:
  Gepetta's house

A retelling of the classic tale, Mississippi Pinocchio *is set on the Mississippi Delta in 1900. PINOCCHIO is the creation of Gepetta, a recently arrived immigrant from Italy. She carved her puppet in hopes of making money by performing with him in the streets. But the puppet has a mind of his own and has escaped his creator. PINOCCHIO has just run away from Gepetta in the street and dodged back into her house. [You might want to create the cricket by an actor manipulating a puppet.]*

PINOCCHIO: Well, what do you know! I got free of that Gepetta lady, lickety-split! Now I'm as free as can be! Causing that much trouble in town makes a puppet hungry. Wonder where I can find me some food?

(PINOCCHIO starts to look around. He hears something.)

CRICKET: Cri-cri-cri.

PINOCCHIO: Who's that?

CRICKET: Cri-cri-cri.

PINOCCHIO: Aw, it's just an ole cricket on the wall.

CRICKET: Who you calling "just"?

PINOCCHIO: Who said that?

CRICKET: I'm "just" about the smartest creature you'll ever meet.

PINOCCHIO: That so.

CRICKET: I've lived in this room nigh on to a hundred years.

PINOCCHIO: Well, it's my room now! Why don't you "just" hop off somewhere else.

CRICKET: You ought to be listening to me. 'Cause I know what I'm talking about.

PINOCCHIO: *(A know-it-all.)* Is that so? Well, say it quick then.

CRICKET: I knew a boy once who ran off to see the world. Had his head all in a whirl, thinking he was the finest thing to come out of a piece of wood. Oh yeah, he said he didn't need school.

PINOCCHIO: Nobody needs school!

CRICKET: He said school was for fools!

PINOCCHIO: He sounds like me!

CRICKET: Just like you.

PINOCCHIO: I'm going to do whatever I want whenever I want it!

CRICKET: Know what that boy grew up to be?

PINOCCHIO: King!

CRICKET: Of the donkeys.

PINOCCHIO: Just like — *(Insulted.)* Hey!

CRICKET: Hee-haw!

PINOCCHIO: I'm not a donkey. I'm growing up to be king of everything!

CRICKET: Hee-haw!

PINOCCHIO: You watch. Let other boys sit in schools and learn stuff, I'll be —

CRICKET: In the hospital or in jail!

PINOCCHIO: You listen here, Cricket. You better take out of here and quick!

CRICKET: You think a wise ole cricket like me is gonna listen to a dumb ole wooden-headed puppet like you??

PINOCCHIO: You ought to.

(PINOCCHIO picks up a book and smashes the cricket.)

PINOCCHIO: There. Least books are good for something! "Grow up to be a donkey." I'll show you! But first, I got to fill my hungry stomach.

(PINOCCHIO begins to exit. He stops for a moment, and turns and looks at the smushed cricket. He feels a hint of remorse. But he shakes it off and goes on along his way.)

End of Scene

REAL, LIKE ME?

Adapted from *Mississippi Pinocchio*

CHARACTERS: (2 m)
   Pinocchio: A wooden puppet who has recently come to
      life
   Lampwick: A tough real boy

SETTING:
   In the woods in Mississippi, 1900.

A retelling of the classic tale, Mississippi Pinocchio *is
set on the Mississippi Delta in 1900. PINOCCHIO has
just escaped the treachery of the Fox and Cat who
tried to hang him from a tree so they could steal his
money. The puppet was rescued by the blue fairy, dis-
guised as a nurse. She has just given him advice on
how to become a real boy and sent him home to his
mother, Gepetta. PINOCCHIO is headed down a path
in the woods. LAMPWICK spots him.*

PINOCCHIO: That nurse-lady said: "Go straight home,
   then find your angel. Or was it, "Find your angel, then
   go straight home?" Angel, home. Home, angel.
LAMPWICK: Where you been, Pine-boy?
PINOCCHIO: Where you been, Lampwick?
LAMPWICK: Asked you first.
PINOCCHIO: I've been to the tip-top of a hickory tree!
LAMPWICK: How's a puppet do that?
PINOCCHIO: Easy!
LAMPWICK: I don't believe you!

PINOCCHIO: I did! I climbed up all by myself!

(PINOCCHIO feels his nose starting to grow and grabs it.)

PINOCCHIO: Wait, nose! Don't grow! I didn't climb up there. I got hung up there by robbers!

(PINOCCHIO checks his nose. It is not growing.)

PINOCCHIO: See! I'm telling the truth.
LAMPWICK: What's wrong with your nose?
PINOCCHIO: Well, it grows when I . . . it's a long story.
LAMPWICK: Robbers, huh. What robbers?
PINOCCHIO: I couldn't see them in the dark. But they left me hanging in that tree. I would of died for sure.
LAMPWICK: So how'd you get down?
PINOCCHIO: Well . . .
LAMPWICK: *(Making fun of him.)* Did you fly?
PINOCCHIO: Naw! It was . . . an angel!

(PINOCCHIO touches his nose. It doesn't grow. He takes this as proof.)

PINOCCHIO: Hah! I *wasn't* dreaming. I knew I'd found me an angel! How 'bout that!
LAMPWICK: What're you talking about? Ain't no such thing!
PINOCCHIO: She *was* an angel, sure as anything!
LAMPWICK: What'd she look like?
PINOCCHIO: I didn't see her . . . exactly.
LAMPWICK: Don't believe in anything you can't see, puppet.
PINOCCHIO: But I know she was there!

(LAMPWICK laughs at him.)

PINOCCHIO: The nurse-lady said that angel can turn me
　　into a real boy!
LAMPWICK: Like me?
PINOCCHIO: I'll be honest and do right —
LAMPWICK: And you'll take what you can get 'cause
　　nobody gives you nothing. That's what this real boy
　　does.
PINOCCHIO: That doesn't sound like the kind of real I've
　　heard about. But, I just got made, you know. Carved
　　out of wood by my momma.
LAMPWICK: Well welcome to the *real* world. You go chas-
　　ing angels, puppet. I'm headed downstream. There's a
　　catfish out in the deepest part of the river. Big as a
　　steam engine. Can swallow you whole. Comes out when
　　it's dark!
PINOCCHIO: *(Scared.)* Really?
LAMPWICK: You scared?
PINOCCHIO: Naw. My angel will protect me — I hope.
LAMPWICK: Hope is for losers. Who do you wanna be,
　　Pinoc? A loser or like me?
PINOCCHIO: I wanna be real.

(LAMPWICK shakes his head.)

LAMPWICK: See ya, Pine-boy.
PINOCCHIO: But . . .

(LAMPWICK exits as PINOCCHIO watches him go.)

PINOCCHIO: Bye.

End of Scene

SEE WHERE YOU LAND

Adapted from *Lift: Icarus and Me*

CHARACTERS: (1 w, 1 m)
Atalanta: 14, an Annie Oakley–like Wild West carnival gal
Lenny: 14, a would-be inventor who dreams of flying

SETTING:
On the dunes of east Texas, 1899.

Lift: Icarus and Me is inspired by the ancient Greek myth of Daedalus and Icarus, as well as the myth of Atalanta. LENNY lives with his grandfather Daedalus, who was once a well-known inventor who created a flying machine. But LENNY's father, Icarus, crashed it and was killed. LENNY was too young to know his father and does not know how he died. But he does have a deep fear of heights. Nevertheless, LENNY, too, longs to fly.

In this scene, LENNY has just pledged to give up his dream of flying even though Minus, a carnival barker, has Daedalus' wrecked plane. LENNY has just taken apart his own invention — a bicycle with wings — and buried it. ATALANTA, his new friend, enters pushing LENNY's bike-plane. ATALANTA works in the carnival for Minus. Minus has told ATALANTA about Icarus' fate.

ATALANTA: Hey Root. Look what I found.

LENNY: *(Lying.)* That ain't mine.

ATALANTA: Guess somebody else made a flappin'-winged
bicycle. Not you — the grandson of a flying genius!

LENNY: Who's scared of heights!

ATALANTA: Everybody's scared of something. What'd you
go and take your invention apart for?

LENNY: 'Cause it's crazy! *(Quoting Grandpa.)* Flying is for
birdbrains!

ATALANTA: *(Reeling him in.)* Guess there's no point, then,
in your trying to fix that amazing aeroplane of your
granddaddy's.

LENNY: Is it broke?

ATALANTA: *(An understatement.)* Oh yeah.

LENNY: How'd it break? What happened?

ATALANTA: You ever ask your granddaddy about that?

LENNY: We never speak of flying.

ATALANTA: Oh. *(Shifting the subject to the bike-plane.)* I
tried to piece this back together, but it don't look right.

LENNY: *(Discovering.)* Hey. You made a tail.

ATALANTA: I did?

LENNY: A tail! Maybe that's what a flying machine needs —
for control!

ATALANTA: Ask your grandpa.

LENNY: We *don't talk* of flying!

ATALANTA: Then sniff it out for yourself — like a hound
dog. Don't you wanna show Minus and everybody else
that your grandpa weren't no fool?!

LENNY: You bet I do.

ATALANTA: Show the world he was a dreamer . . . like you.

*(LENNY smiles. Everybody needs a friend like ATA-
LANTA.)*

LENNY: Well . . . If we could find the drawings Grandpa
    made of his inventions —
ATALANTA: Where's he keep them?
LENNY: *(Realizing.)* Must be in that secret trunk of his.
ATALANTA: So get 'em.
LENNY: From the attic? I can't climb that high!
ATALANTA: Sure you can.
LENNY: Even if I could fix his aeroplane, I'd be scared to
    fly way . . . *(Looking up at the sky.)* up there.
ATALANTA: Aw, just jump off a cliff!
LENNY: Pardon me?
ATALANTA: Take a running jump and see where you land.
    Take a chance, Root.
LENNY: I'm "Root," remember. I'm stuck on the ground!
ATALANTA: That ain't your real name, is it?

(LENNY doesn't say.)

ATALANTA: Come on, now. Is it?
LENNY: Naw. It's "Lenny." After Leonardo da Vinci, the
    I-talian inventor. But nobody calls me that.
ATALANTA: Your grandpa will, soon as he sees his flying
    machine come back to life!

(LENNY hesitates.)

ATALANTA: You can do it, "Lenny." Or at least try.
LENNY: You're a pal, Atalanta.
ATLANTA: You bet I am.
LENNY: Meet me tonight at midnight, all right?
ATALANTA: Atta boy. Midnight.

(They shake on it.)

End of Scene

HAPPY LANDING

Adapted from *Lift: Icarus and Me*

CHARACTERS: (1 w, 1 m)
    Atlanta: 14
    Lenny: 14

SETTING:
    Lenny's house, on the dunes of east Texas, 1899.

    Lift: Icarus and Me *is inspired by the ancient Greek myth of Daedalus and Icarus, as well as the myth of Atalanta. (See page 104 for story description.)*

    In this scene, LENNY and ATALANTA are trying to find the plans that LENNY's grandfather, Daedalus, made for his flying machine inventions. It is midnight. Daedalus is asleep. LENNY cautiously climbs the ladder toward Daedalus' trunk, which is just out of his reach.

LENNY: Am I there yet?
ATALANTA: Just keep your eyes closed.
LENNY: I gotta see where to hold on!
ATALANTA: No you don't. Just get it.

    (LENNY wobbles on the ladder, but he manages to get the trunk and start back down.)

ATALANTA: Steady now.

(LENNY plops the trunk down, triumphantly.)

LENNY: *(Pleased with himself.)* How 'bout that.
ATALANTA: You got the key?
LENNY: *(Putting the key in the lock.)* Slipped it right out of
    where he hides it.
ATALANTA: You're catchin' on, boy.

*(LENNY opens the trunk and pulls out a roll of
mechanical drawings.)*

LENNY: Great golly, would you looka here.
ATALANTA: Bull's-eye!

*(They pour through pages of the big drawings. LENNY
can't believe it.)*

ATALANTA: How many flying machines can a man dream
    up? *(Pointing to one.)* Sure as shootin' that's ours. Now
    you can fix that aeroplane and make it fly!
LENNY: *(Studying the drawing.)* He didn't make the wings
    to flap. But no tail. Huh.
ATALANTA: Bet that's your daddy in the pilot seat.
LENNY: Can't be. My daddy never flew.

(ATLANTA looks puzzled.)

LENNY: Grandpa said.
ATALANTA: He said that? Oh.
LENNY: *(Looking closely at the drawing.)* Wonder who
    that is?

*(ATALANTA is pretty sure that it is LENNY's father,
Icarus.)*

ATALANTA: Tell you what. You sneak off tomorrow afternoon. I'll get past Minus and meet you on the dune
where she's put the machine. There's this big ladder
you climb.
LENNY: *(Couldn't be worse.)* Perfect.
ATALANTA: Just 'cause your daddy fell — *(Stopping herself.)* You won't fall, Lenny.

*(ATALANTA pulls a set of pilot's goggles from the
trunk.)*

ATALANTA: Bet these pilot's goggles were your daddy's — I
mean, your granddaddy's, too. Take them. You're gonna
need them.
LENNY: I gotta fix Grandpa's aeroplane before I can fly it. *If*
I can fly it. Leave them here.
ATALANTA: Suit yourself.

*(ATALANTA turns to go, but LENNY takes her hand,
friendly, but maybe a little more.)*

LENNY: Thanks.
ATALANTA: Happy landing!

*(They release hands. LENNY looks back at the plans.
ATALANTA slips the goggles into her pocket.)*

ATALANTA: G'night.

(She exits. LENNY watches her go.)

End of Scene

FOR MY FATHER

Adapted from *The Odyssey of Telémaca*

CHARACTERS: (1 w, 1 m)
　　Telémaca: 14
　　Hérmio: 14

SETTING:
　　The Sonoran Desert at the turn of the twentieth century

　　The Odyssey of Telémaca *resets* Homer's Odyssey *in Mexico. Omero [Odysseus] is a hero of the people, defending the land of the peasants from the rich. He has been gone for many years. TELÉMACA, his daughter, has set out to find him. She is hiding, having been pursued into the desert by El Rico, a villainous landowner. Thinking she is finally safe, TELÉMACA creeps out from her hiding place. But she meets a single bright light emerging from the darkness.*

TELÉMACA: Ahhh! A one-eyed spirit!
HÉRMIO: No, I have two.

　　(HÉRMIO stands, holding a lantern. TELÉMACA draws her sword.)

TELÉMACA: *(Holding him at sword-point.)* If you are loyal to El Rico then you are my enemy.

HÉRMIO: I am loyal to the memory of my father. *(Politely.)* Could you put that down?

TELÉMACA: Who was your father?

HÉRMIO: He fought alongside the great Omero. But he died in battle.

TELÉMACA: *(Putting down her sword.) Lo siento.*

HÉRMIO: Now I walk in the steps of my father. He was a *curandero.* I will heal our land from El Rico.

TELÉMACA: How?

HÉRMIO: By faith and skill. I have much faith and . . . I'm working on the skill. *(Pulling a pouch out of his bag.)* I search the desert for ingredients for my charms.

(TELÉMACA jumps onto a rock and swooshes her sword impressively.)

TELÉMACA: I search for my father. Only he can save my mamá and our *pueblo!*

HÉRMIO: *Impresionante!* You sure *you* can't save everybody?

TELÉMACA: I'm not my father! Do you have a charm that can tell me where he is or . . . if he lives?

HÉRMIO: I'm a beginner. *(Getting an idea.)* What you need is a spirit. A ghost who dwells between the living and the dead. *(Indicating his bag.)* I don't have one of those.

TELÉMACA: *(Struck by a plan.)* La Llorona.

HÉRMIO: *Cómo?*

TELÉMACA: She once lived but now haunts the night.

HÉRMIO: *(Frightened.)* And drags you to the bottom of the river if you cross her path! *¿Estas loca?*

TELÉMACA: I will find her, so I might find my *papá —*

(TELÉMACA takes out a photo and shows it to HÉRMIO.)

HÉRMIO: The great Omero! You are his daughter Telémaca?
TELÉMACA: Sí.
HÉRMIO: *(Thrilled.) Qué va!*
TELÉMACA: *Cómo?*
HÉRMIO: I am Hérmio. "Hermito." The son of Hérmio, el *Curandero*.
TELÉMACA: You are *that* Hérmio?
HÉRMIO: Sí. My father spoke of you . . . and our future . . . a lot!
TELÉMACA: And mine of you.

(An awkward moment as they realize they've just met the person they are supposed to marry.)

TELÉMACA: I should go.
HÉRMIO: I'll go with you.
TELÉMACA: *(Starting to go.)* No, *gracias.*
HÉRMIO: Then I'll wait for you.
TELÉMACA: I don't need any help.
HÉRMIO: But you might need a *curandero*. Wait! *Por favor!*

(TELÉMACA stops. He reaches into his bag, searching for a pouch.)

HÉRMIO: I know it's here somewh — Ah! Take this pouch. What's inside will protect you on your journey.

(TELÉMACA takes the pouch, opens it but closes it quickly.)

TELÉMACA: A cricket?!!
HÉRMIO: You never know. I told you. I'm a beginner.
TELÉMACA: Adiós, Hérmio.

(TELÉMACA and HÉRMIO walk away from each other to exit. First HÉRMIO turns and looks back at TELÉMACA, but she is not looking. Then TELÉMACA looks back at him, but HÉRMIO does not see. HÉRMIO finally exits. TELÉMACA looks after him once he is gone. She holds the pouch to her heart, then puts it in her pocket and exits.)

End of Scene

To help you with the language and culture in the scene:

Lo siento: Means "I'm sorry."

Curandero: A person from traditional Mexican culture who is a healer, using plants and other ingredients from the natural world

Pueblo: Means "village" in this scene

Impresionante!: Means "very impressive!"

Cómo?: Means "What did you say?"

La Llorona: A ghost from Mexican legend who wanders the night, crying, searching for her lost children. Parents sometimes frighten their children into going to sleep at night or warn them not to go out into the night alone because of *La Llorona.*

¿Estas loca?: Means "Are you crazy?"

Sí: Means "yes."

Qué va!: An expression meaning "This is great!" or "How lucky is this!"

Gracias: Means "thank you."

Por favor: Means "please."

Adios: Means "good-bye."

CHAPTER FIVE

Scenes for Four Actors

(5 – 10 minutes)

THE AUDITION

Adapted from *What Part Will I Play?*

CHARACTERS: (4 w)
    Jessie: 10 - 12
    Amy: 10 - 12
    Tiffany: 11 - 13
    Brittany: 11 - 13

SETTING:
    On an empty stage of a theater

    Four girls have arrived in a theater to audition for a play. But the stage manager tells them that they have to wait for the arrival of the director and playwright. The stage manager has just exited into the light booth.

JESSIE: What did the stage manager say?

AMY: "Wait." We have to wait to audition.

TIFFANY: *(Quoting the Stage Manager.)* "Spend some time getting to know each other." How weird is that?

BRITTANY: *(Calling up to the tech booth.)* Look, sir, we came here to audition. Why do we have to wait? *(No answer.)* Hello! *(Silence from the booth.)*

TIFFANY: Completely weird.

JESSIE: Guess we're waiting.

    (The girls wait. It is awkward.)

TIFFANY: Like, we're supposed to be . . . with each other?

AMY: He said it wouldn't be long.

JESSIE: Does this always happen at an audition, Brittany? Bet you've been to millions of them.

BRITTANY: This *never* happens.

(The girls wait again.)

AMY: Maybe they're still writing the play.

JESSIE: Yeah, and they don't know what parts there'll be yet.

BRITTANY: There's always a lead.

TIFFANY: And that's always you?

(BRITTANY glares at TIFFANY, who glares right back.)

JESSIE: I've seen her in thousands of shows!

AMY: Really?

JESSIE: OK, *lots*. You're really good, Brittany.

TIFFANY: A real star.

BRITTANY: Thanks.

(BRITTANY crosses away from the other three girls and sits by herself. An awkward pause as the girls are unsure of what to do next.)

TIFFANY: So.

JESSIE: We could tell jokes.

AMY: I can never remember any. You tell one.

JESSIE: I don't know any, either. I was just trying to be funny! That's my usual part . . . in life.

AMY: In a play I'm usually the maid or a tree, some really small part.

JESSIE: I'm always a boy.

TIFFANY: I'm *never* a boy. I wish I had my phone.

JESSIE: I wish I *had* a phone.

TIFFANY: I could at least call my boyfriend.

JESSIE: You've got one of those, too?

TIFFANY: Sure. We meet at the mall. Go to parties. I don't spend my whole life being in plays, like some people.

(TIFFANY throws a look at BRITTANY. BRITTANY does not respond.)

AMY: My mom doesn't let me have a boyfriend. But she does like me to have boy friends. Sometimes I'll tease her and ask, "So what makes a boy a boyfriend?" Then she'll tell me stories all about her first dates!

JESSIE: Your *mom* does that?

AMY: Sure.

JESSIE: But she's your mom. Moms don't do things like that.

AMY: Mine does.

JESSIE: That's amazing.

AMY: We're good friends. It's always been just the two of us.

TIFFANY: Your parents divorced?

AMY: Since I was two.

JESSIE: You happy, Mr. Stage Manager? We're getting to know each other. *(No reply.)*

BRITTANY: He's not listening.

TIFFANY: But you are. That's a surprise.

JESSIE: *(To AMY.)* So, no brothers or sisters?

AMY: Nope.

TIFFANY and JESSIE: Lucky!

JESSIE: My brother is eight. Get this, *eight!* And when he destroys the house or almost kills the dog or something, my mom goes, "Oh, he's only eight. He doesn't know any better." She would have killed me if I'd done something that bad when I was eight.

AMY: What are your parents like, Tiffany?

TIFFANY: They're great.

JESSIE: I knew it.

TIFFANY: I mean, I guess they're great. I don't have a lot of time to spend with them. You have to make a choice if you want to have a social life. And I'd rather have friends, you know?

JESSIE: Uh . . . sure.

AMY: Sometimes my mom tries *too* hard to be my friend. To be the "open-minded" parent. Like the other day, I came in with my new outfit on and I said, "So what do you think, Mom?" And she goes, "It's cute. It's a little tight and not exactly the right color for you. But if *you* want to wear it, it's *your* choice." What am I suppose to do when she says that?

JESSIE: "Thanks, Mom. I think I'll wear it for the rest of my life."

TIFFANY: You *are* funny, Jessie.

JESSIE: *(Liking the attention from TIFFANY.)* Thanks.

TIFFANY: Last week I got invited to a party, but I haven't told my mom yet because I know she'd use it. If I don't pick up my room or do my homework, I'd hear, "You won't be going to that party if you don't do what I say." So I won't tell her until two days before. Then I'll act really perfect until Friday night. I can handle that for forty-eight hours!

JESSIE: My parents expect me to be perfect twenty-four hours a day for the rest of my life. What's the point? How can you have any fun if you're perfect?

TIFFANY: Ask Brittany.

(AMY crosses away from the other two girls, trying to engage BRITTANY in the conversation.)

AMY: Brittany, what are your parents like? I bet they come to all your shows.

JESSIE: Bring you flowers. Brag about you all the time.

BRITTANY: Sometimes.

JESSIE: Oh, come on. If my kid were as talented as you, I'd wear a sign or something: "Mother of Brittany Taylor."

BRITTANY: She's got her own life. So does my dad. And I've got mine. So we're even.

TIFFANY: They both work?

BRITTANY: We're all busy people. That's just the way it is.

AMY: My mom says you have to make time to be together.

BRITTANY: Well my mom doesn't say that, OK?

AMY: Sorry.

BRITTANY: Don't be sorry.

AMY: No, I mean I'm sorry for saying that. Not for . . .

BRITTANY: I know what you mean.

(It is silent for a moment among the girls.)

TIFFANY: They never come to see you? Ever?

(BRITTANY shrugs, not really saying, but the girls begin to understand. Nobody moves or says anything, then JESSIE crosses to the booth.)

JESSIE: *(Looking up at the booth.)* Hello? Mr. Stage Manager?

AMY: Hey, that light wasn't on before. Maybe he's back.

JESSIE: With a finished script!

AMY: Let's line up. Maybe there's a part for all of us.

(JESSIE and AMY line up. Neither TIFFANY nor BRIT-TANY moves.)

BRITTANY: That's not how it works.
JESSIE: It might. This time.
AMY: Maybe this play will be different.
TIFFANY: For all of us. *(Crossing to BRITTANY.)* You want to go first?
BRITTANY: You can.
TIFFANY: Can we go together?

(BRITTANY crosses with TIFFANY and joins the line.)

JESSIE: *(To the booth.)* We're ready.

End of Scene

FINDERS KEEPERS?

CHARACTERS: (2 w, 2 m)
    Alison: 12 - 13
    Maya: 12 - 13
    Elijah: 12 - 13
    Brendan: 12 - 13

SETTING:
    At the mall

    Four friends have just gotten out of the last showing of a movie at the mall. They are waiting for the bus.

MAYA: If you guys ever ask me to go see a movie as scary as that again, I swear I'll never speak to you!
ELIJAH: Promise?
ALISON: You are so rude.
ELIJAH: *(Laughing.)* It wasn't that scary.
MAYA and ALISON: Yes it was.
BRENDAN: What, you didn't like the part where the guy jumped up out of the grave?

    (BRENDAN jumps toward the girls, imitating the moment.)

BRENDAN: Aaah!
MAYA and ALISON: AAAAHHH!
ALISON: Quit it, Brendan!
MAYA: *(Liking being scared.)* Do it again.
BRENDAN: AAAAHHH!

ELIJAH: Hey, they arrest kids for screaming at the mall.

ALISON: They arrest boys!

BRENDAN: Where's the bus?

ALISON: I've never been here this late.

MAYA: Wow. All the stores are closed!

ELIJAH: Will Maya the shopaholic survive?

MAYA: Don't be stupid.

ALISON: There *is* one more bus, right?

ELIJAH: I take it home all the time.

ALISON: Your parents give you a lot of freedom.

ELIJAH: I deserve it.

MAYA: *(Skeptically.)* Really?

(BRENDAN crosses to something he has spotted on the ground.)

ELIJAH: Mom tells me all the time: "You have such good judgment, Elijah."

MAYA: Boy, have you got her fooled!

BRENDAN: Hey guys. Look.

(BRENDAN picks up a wallet from the ground.)

ALISON: Look at that.

BRENDAN: Somebody dropped their wallet.

MAYA: Who's is it?

BRENDAN: How should I know?

ALISON: Open it. Check for an ID.

(BRENDAN opens it.)

BRENDAN: *(Looking through it.)* No cards. Nothing. Except money. *(He counts it quickly.)* Fifty dollars.

MAYA: Put it back where you found it.

ELIJAH: And have somebody else find it and take the money? No way.

MAYA: Whoever dropped it will come back for it.

ALISON: Maybe.

MAYA: Alison. We can't take the money.

ALISON: I didn't say we should.

BRENDAN: I found it.

ELIJAH: But it was my idea to come to the movies. We'll split it.

MAYA: You guys!

ELIJAH: Finders keepers!

BRENDAN: Losers weepers?

ALISON: But it's fifty dollars.

BRENDAN: We could call the police.

MAYA: Or give it to somebody in the movie theater. The ticket guy or somebody.

BRENDAN: So *he* can take the money?

ELIJAH: No way!

ALISON: So he can keep it safe till the owner comes back to claim it.

MAYA: Exactly!

BRENDAN: OK. That's worth a try.

(BRENDAN crosses to the cinema door and pulls on it.)

BRENDAN: It's locked.

ALISON: Knock!

BRENDAN: *(Knocking.)* Hello? Hello!

ELIJAH: He's vacuuming the floor or something. He can't hear you.

ALISON and MAYA: *(Knocking.)* Hello?!!

MAYA: Nothing.

ALISON: And we can't leave it at a store.

MAYA: They're closed.

(The four kids are quiet for a moment. No one is sure what to do next.)

ELIJAH: I say we split it four ways.

BRENDAN: Elijah!

ELIJAH: Be honest, guys. You all want to take it. Somebody's going to take it. Why shouldn't it be us?

BRENDAN: He's got a point.

MAYA: But it's not ours!

ALISON: OK. We'll take it.

MAYA: What?

ALISON: Have you got any paper, Maya?

MAYA: Just my diary.

ALISON: Rip out a page.

ELIJAH: What for?

ALISON: To write a note. We'll take the money, but we'll leave the wallet with a note.

BRENDAN: Saying what exactly?

ALISON: To call — *(She looks around the group.)* one of us. If the person can tell us exactly how much money was in the wallet, we'll give it back to them.

MAYA: You're a genius, Alison.

BRENDAN: What if they just guess and get it right?

MAYA: That won't happen.

ELIJAH: It might.

MAYA: I bet Elijah will call you, Alison.

BRENDAN: *(Doing an exaggerated voice.)* "Hello. I lost fifty dollars at the movies."

ELIJAH: I won't.

MAYA: You might.

BRENDAN: I'll hang on to the money.

MAYA: It was Alison's idea. She should keep it.

ALISON: I'm putting my e-mail address. *(She writes.)* There. *(She puts the note in the wallet.)* Let's put it up on this ledge to make it easier for the owner to spot. OK. Done.

(The four kids look at the wallet.)

MAYA: What if nobody e-mails you?

ELIJAH: Yeah. What then?

BRENDAN: Then we split it four ways. Fair?

ELIJAH: OK by me.

MAYA: Maybe.

BRENDAN: Alison?

ELIJAH: She'll give her share to charity or something. You watch!

MAYA: Alison, if nobody claims it . . .

ALISON: OK. Four ways. The Animal Rescue League can do a lot with $12.50.

ELIJAH: And *I* can buy a lot of I-tunes!

BRENDAN: We can all do what we want.

ALISON: *If* nobody e-mails.

MAYA: There's the bus.

BRENDAN: Let's go.

ALISON: Sure hope somebody e-mails.

MAYA: Soon.

BRENDAN: Yeah, by Monday.

ELIJAH: By tomorrow!

MAYA: Monday!

ELIJAH: No way!

ALISON: Quick, the bus!

BRENDAN: Come on!
ELIJAH: Bye wallet.

(The four kids hurry toward the bus and get on.)

End of Scene

GO CONSTITUTION!

CHARACTERS: (2 w, 2 m)
  Matilda: 11 - 13
  Grace: 11 - 13
  Aaron: 11 - 13
  Jahan: 11 - 13

SETTING:
  Their classroom

  MATILDA is the editor of the school newspaper.
  GRACE and AARON write for the paper and JAHAN
  draws the paper's cartoons. MATILDA, AARON, and
  JAHAN are behind on finding a lead story for this
  Friday's paper. They are in the midst of a planning
  meeting, right before school.

AARON: I've got it, guys. I'll write a feature story on the
  new playground equipment.
MATILDA: We've already written about that.
JAHAN: Remember? I did three cartoons of people falling
  off the new spinning thing.
MATILDA: Which is why the PTA got us a different piece of
  equipment. *(Raising her fist.)* Power of the press!
AARON, MATILDA, and JAHAN: *(Group high five.)* Power
  of the press!
JAHAN: We could write about the fifth grade's class trip.
MATILDA: A fifth grader should write that, but none of
  them are ready for the front page.
AARON: Yeah.

JAHAN: Nico's pretty good. He wrote that article about the secret life of hissing roaches.

MATILDA: That was weird.

JAHAN: It was cool!

MATILDA: I'm the editor! I say it was weird. So it was weird.

JAHAN: OK, fine.

AARON: Come on. We can't have a big blank hole on the front of Friday's paper.

MATILDA: Where's my folder? Let's check the story list we brainstormed at the beginning of the year —

(GRACE comes rushing into the room. She's wearing a basketball team shirt, which fits awkwardly.)

AARON: Grace, where've you been? We've got a crisis here.

JAHAN: No front-page story!

(GRACE is trying to catch her breath.)

MATILDA: You OK? You're all out of breath.

JAHAN: Bet she ran up the stairs.

AARON: What's up with the basketball shirt? You're not on the team.

GRACE: It's what our principal gave me to wear.

MATILDA, AARON, and JAHAN: Huh? / What?

GRACE: When he made me take off the shirt I wore to school today! I walked through the front door and he said, "Into my office, Grace Peters."

MATILDA: Was your midriff showing?

JAHAN: Dress-code violation!

GRACE: It was a T-shirt! A big one.

AARON: So what was the problem?

GRACE: He didn't like what was written on it.

JAHAN: Was it swearing?

GRACE: No. It said "Save the trees. Stop the high-rise."

AARON: What's the problem with that?

MATILDA: That's on signs all over the neighborhood. Mom says nobody likes what those developers are planning.

GRACE: Well somebody does.

JAHAN: Our principal?

GRACE: He didn't say that exactly. But he said my shirt would be "disruptive to the school environment." He won't let me protest on school grounds! I have my rights, you know.

MATILDA: Yeah, that's not fair.

AARON: Have we got a story now!

MATILDA: You are so right. Remember Social Studies? We were studying the Constitution —

JAHAN: The Bill of Rights!

MATILDA: And there were those school kids protesting the Vietnam war.

GRACE: I'm just protesting a building!

MATILDA: They wanted to wear black armbands with a peace sign, but the principal forbid it. So they sued! Their case went all the way to the Supreme Court.

AARON: Did they win?

GRACE and MATILDA: Yes!

JAHAN: Get a lawyer, Grace. Quick.

GRACE: I just want to wear my shirt! It's a free country.

JAHAN: Not at school.

MATILDA: Sure it is.

JAHAN: Aren't schools different? With their own rules?

MATILDA: School rules shouldn't stop your rights. Right?

GRACE, JAHAN, and AARON: *(Another high five.)* Right!

JAHAN: I can see a cartoon forming in my mind!

AARON: And I've got the headline —

MATILDA: I'm the editor, but go ahead.

AARON: "Middle Schooler Denied Her Freedom of Speech by a Tree-Hating Principal."

JAHAN: That's libel!

AARON: What?

JAHAN: You can't publish something false about a person.

AARON: But it's true!

MATILDA: We don't *know* that he's a tree-hater.

GRACE: He must be. Why else wouldn't he let me wear my shirt?

JAHAN: Not everybody wants to save the trees.

(The other three kids turn and look at JAHAN in disbe-lief.)

JAHAN: The developer guys sure don't. Maybe the principal's brother is a developer or his mother or something.

GRACE: Then he can wear a T-shirt that says "Kill the Trees."

AARON: I'd rip it off him!

MATILDA: Great. Physically attack a person because of his beliefs. That's when the Constitution doesn't protect you anymore.

AARON: It doesn't?

MATILDA: Didn't you read *anything* in Social Studies this year?

AARON: I . . . skimmed it.

GRACE: I have a right to my opinion. It doesn't hurt any-body. I should be able to express it anywhere I want. School included.

JAHAN: You write the article, Grace.

AARON: Yeah!

GRACE: I really want to, guys, but . . .

MATILDA: But what?

GRACE: I don't want to get into any more trouble.

MATILDA: We'll just report the facts. No opinions, Aaron. Just the facts. We've got freedom of the press!

JAHAN: Even at school?

MATILDA: I think so.

GRACE: I hope so.

(GRACE takes a beat, looking at all her friends.)

GRACE: OK. I'll have it finished by lunchtime.

MATILDA: *(Raising her fist.)* Go Constitution!

ALL: Go Constitution!

(Group high five.)

End of Scene

FOUR SQUARE

CHARACTERS: (4 w)
    Winnie: 10
    Penny: 10
    Celia: 10
    Ella: 10

SETTING:
    In a schoolyard, 1940.

WINNIE, PENNY, and CELIA are school friends who meet every morning before the bell rings to play four square. ELLA, who lives on Gibson Hill, is new to the school and is ignored by the other children. WINNIE, PENNY, and CELIA rush on, drop their books, and cross to their places on the four-square. ELLA watches them, standing at a distance. [The challenge in this scene is to keep the game going under the girls' dialogue.]

PENNY: Why'd you make us wait, Winnie?
CELIA: She's always a little late.
WINNIE: *(Holding the ball.)* Let's play four square.
CELIA: If we have time before the bell rings.
PENNY: *(Calling her place in the game.)* King.
CELIA: Queen.
WINNIE: OK. Knight.

(WINNIE notices ELLA standing alone and looks at the empty fourth place in the square.)

PENNY: Gimme the ball!

(WINNIE quickly turns her back on ELLA and throws the ball to PENNY.)

PENNY: *(She begins to pass the ball.)* I know just what we can do after school.
WINNIE: How about we walk up Gibson Hill?
CELIA: What for?
PENNY: That's silly.
CELIA: There're no wildflowers up there in October.
PENNY: Exactly. Out of the woods!

(All the girls jump outside the four-square.)

WINNIE: We might just want to see who — what's up there.
PENNY: You won't catch me up there till next spring. That road cakes your shoes with mud. Bus stop.

(Each girls puts a foot on the center of the four-square. ELLA shyly looks at her shoes to see if she has mud on them.)

CELIA: Who'd live up there?
PENNY: Not me.
WINNIE: Me neither.
PENNY: Corner!

(Each girl puts a foot on a corner.)

ALL GIRLS: Safe!
PENNY: Your foot didn't touch in time.
CELIA: Yes it did.

PENNY: No it didn't!
WINNIE: Let's just do it again.
PENNY: Round the world!

(PENNY tosses the ball to CELIA, who tosses it to WIN-NIE but she misses.)

PENNY: You're out!
CELIA: I want to be King.
PENNY: Then get me out!

(The ball rolls toward ELLA, who catches it. WINNIE turns to retrieve the ball. ELLA smiles at WINNIE hopefully. WINNIE takes the ball from ELLA, not crossing back into the game.)

PENNY: Come on, Winnie, before the bell!

(WINNIE jumps back into the game. ELLA steps back into her watching place.)

WINNIE: Line!

(Girls race to put a foot on a line of the four-square.)

GIRLS: Safe!
PENNY: I say we go to the picture show.
CELIA: I've got a quarter.
WINNIE: Me, too.
CELIA: You didn't last week.
WINNIE: Yes, I did.
PENNY: Around the world peacefully.

(They toss the ball in a circle, gently.)

CELIA: What if Miss Madison gives us too much homework?

PENNY: She said she never gives homework on Thursday.
And I always believe her.

CELIA: Maybe today they'll show *two* cartoons before the
picture.

PENNY: It'd better be Mickey Mouse. Don't you love Mickey
Mouse, Winnie?

WINNIE: Sure. But . . . I'll just meet you at the pictures.

(Bell rings.)

WINNIE: There's the bell.

*(Girls rush to pick up their things to go into school.
ELLA hangs back.)*

CELIA: *(To PENNY.)* Bet Winnie's going to go up to Gibbons
Hill to see her new little friend.

*(CELIA and PENNY look at ELLA. ELLA looks away
from them.)*

WINNIE: What are you whispering?

PENNY: Wouldn't you like to know.

CELIA: Be sure to wipe the mud off your shoes.

WINNIE: What mud?

PENNY: Now I won't have to bother saving you a seat at the
movies. Come on, Celia.

WINNIE: I said I'd meet you there. Hey, Penny. Wait up.

(PENNY and CELIA shriek with laughter and run into school. ELLA takes a step toward WINNIE, but WINNIE looks away and walks quickly into the school. Now alone, ELLA crosses to the four-square. She stands in a square and moves her foot on and off a line, imagining she's playing. The school bell rings again. ELLA walks into the school alone.)

End of Scene

FOLLOW THE WIND

A Creation Myth from Ancient Arabia

CHARACTERS: (4 w or m)
    Dove
    Partridge
    Sheikh Amal
    Crow

SETTING:
    The desert

*All cultures have stories about how things came to be.
This scene is based on an ancient story from Arabia,
which includes present-day Iraq. [Actors should
always be in character and in the moment of the
action, even when they are speaking in the third person. They should not step out of character to be narra-
tors.]*

DOVE: In the beginning long ago, there was a sheikh of an
    ancient tribe in the Arabian Desert. His name was
    Amal.
PARTRIDGE: He followed the wind and the water to find
    the best land to graze his herd of camels.
DOVE: But one winter night, Amal was very worried.

(DOVE and PARTRIDGE fly to AMAL.)

AMAL: We have no more water and no more pasture to
    graze. Soon my camels will die. Our families will starve.
PARTRIDGE: Let us help you, Amal.
AMAL: How can a bird so small, a partridge, help a Sheikh
    with his troubles?
PARTRIDGE: With gladness in my heart.
DOVE: And power in my wings.
AMAL: You, little dove, also wish to help?
DOVE: We have wandered the desert with you. So we are
    brothers. Aren't we, crow?

(CROW is grumpily sitting away from the others.)

PARTRIDGE: Crow?!
CROW: Don't bother me. I'm looking for something to eat.
    Squawk!!
DOVE: We are all hungry, brother Crow.
PARTRIDGE: That is why we must help our Sheikh.
CROW: How can a bird help a Sheikh? How can a bird help
    himself? I'm starving!
AMAL: Many thanks, my friends. But as leader of our tribe,
    I must scout the countryside to see where our next
    home might be.
PARTRIDGE: But we can scout for you.
DOVE: Your three birds will follow the wind, each in a dif-
    ferent direction.
PARTRIDGE: We can look from a great height and spot our
    next home.
AMAL: Well . . . your wings can carry you much faster than
    my camel can walk.
DOVE: And we will return by day's end. Are you ready,
    Crow?
PARTRIDGE: Crow?!

CROW: I heard you already. Squawk! I'll fly anywhere if I can find some food!

AMAL: I will turn my eyes toward heaven until you return.

DOVE: I will fly north.

PARTRIDGE: And I to the west.

CROW: And I'll go . . . the other way.

(The birds fly off.)

AMAL: So the partridge, the dove, and the crow flew off each in his own direction high up over the desert. Amal waited eagerly for their safe return.

(Each bird stops in his own space, as if hovering in three different places.)

DOVE: The dove soon found rich pasturelands.

PARTRIDGE: And the partridge spied streams with sparkling water.

CROW: And the crow saw acres and acres of rich, wonderful, bountiful land! Look at *that!* He wanted them all for himself! I've got to get back to that Sheikh first.

(The CROW takes off for home.)

AMAL: Sooner than he expected, Amal saw the crow racing toward him.

CROW: Have I got news!

AMAL: Tell me, brother Crow.

CROW: There's nothing.

AMAL: Nothing?

CROW: Not a drop of water or a blade of grass as far as the eye can see.

AMAL: Nothing.

CROW: Sad but true. So we should all stay right here. Of course, I'll be happy to go out and eat — uh, *scout* what might be out there again, but our tribe should just stay put.

AMAL: My hopes were so high.

CROW: Life is tough in the desert for man or crow.

(The DOVE and PARTRIDGE arrive.)

DOVE: Sheikh Amal, I have found a paradise.

PARTRIDGE: As have I!

CROW: Squawk!! Don't listen to those two. The sun's gotten to them. They're imagining things!

DOVE: You are wrong, brother Crow. I saw a land with grass so soft that it could cradle a newborn baby.

PARTRIDGE: And I saw flowing streams of water as clear and cool as diamonds sparkling in the sun.

CROW: Yep. Definitely having a mirage. Both of them. Can't trust little birds, you know.

AMAL: No more! Which report is true and which is false? This is the judgment I must make as Sheikh.

ALL BIRDS: But —

AMAL: Silence!

(The three birds are silent as the sheikh circles around them.)

AMAL: We will go to the land of the dove. Let us see first if the dove speaks the truth.

DOVE: So Amal and his tribe moved their tents and their camels across the golden sand until they found the land that the dove had promised.

AMAL: As thanks for your truthfulness, Dove, I will stain your feet with henna, so that all will know that the pink-footed dove led our tribe and our descendants to a fertile new land.

PARTRIDGE: And when it was time to move again, Amal took his tribe and camels to the land that the Partridge had found.

AMAL: As thanks to you, Partridge, I will ring your eye with the color of a rich jewel — the opal — so that all will know that the ringed-eye partridge spied a plentiful land for our tribe. As for you, Crow —

CROW: Uh, me??

AMAL: For your lie, your color will forever be the color of night so that all will know of the darkness of your lie and your wicked selfishness.

CROW: Can I still have something to eat?

AMAL: Off with you!

CROW: I'm going. I'm going!

(The CROW flies off.)

DOVE: The Bedouin people still live in the deserts of the Arab Peninsula today.

PARTRIDGE: Following the wind, the water —

DOVE and PARTRIDGE: And the birds.

End of Scene

QUIEN BUSCA, HALLA
(He Who Searches, Finds)

Adapted from *The Odyssey of Telémaca*

CHARACTERS: (3 w, 1 m)
   TELÉMACA: 13 - 14
   TOMÁS: 13 - 14
   BLANCA: 13 - 14
   ROSAMARIA: 13 - 14

SETTING:
   The marketplace of a small village in Mexico, 1910.

   The Odyssey of Telémaca *resets Homer's* Odyssey *in Mexico. Omero [Odysseus] is a hero of the people, an almost magical farmer who once made the land plentiful. But he has been gone for many years. He left to defend the land from greedy men like the rich El Rico. TELÉMACA, Omero's daughter, struggles to take her father's place in the village. In this scene, she is in the marketplace where she sells her corn with her friend, TOMÁS. BLANCA and ROSAMARIA, two girls from the village, stand nearby listening.*

TELÉMACA: Look, Tomás. This is all the corn I have to sell. Why has the land become so hard?
TOMÁS: It misses your *papá*.
TELÉMACA: Did you meet the postman this morning?
TOMÁS: Yes.

TELÉMACA: And you are sure there was no letter for me?

TOMÁS: Not today.

TELÉMACA: Not for five years!

TOMÁS: I'm sorry, Telémaca. Everyone in the *pueblo* prays for Omero's return.

TELÉMACA: No one more than I. *(Trying to cheer up.)* So, how would you like to buy some corn?

TOMÁS: My pockets are empty. And so is my stomach.

TELÉMACA: *(Pulling out a coin.)* Here. Go buy us some *pan dulce* from the baker.

TOMÁS: But you have so little money —

TELÉMACA: Come back with it soon and I'll tell you stories of my *papá*.

TOMÁS: *Gracias*, Telémaca. I will run like the wind and back again.

(TOMÁS races off.)

TELÉMACA: *(Calling after him.)* Just make sure you save some sweet cakes for me!

(BLANCA and ROSAMARIA cross to TELÉMACA.)

TELÉMACA: *Maíz, señoritas?* Sweet corn?

BLANCA: Your father grew corn of gold. But look at it now!

ROSAMARIA: Soon nothing will grow.

BLANCA: Without Omero.

TELÉMACA: I've tried to make the maíz grow. And if I could bring more water from the mountain springs to our fields, I would!

ROSAMARIA: Your father could.

BLANCA: *He* was a hero.

ROSAMARIA: But you?

BLANCA: My mamá says a child can never fill a man's shoes.

TELÉMACA: I can. I will!

ROSAMARIA: Without Omero, El Rico will take our land! Like he has taken the land in the mountains, the land by the river.

TELÉMACA: No!

BLANCA: Who will defend our *pueblo*? You?

(TELÉMACA is silent.)

ROSAMARIA: How could your father abandon us?

BLANCA: Maybe he is lost in the desert night!

ROSAMARIA: Or frightened to death by *La Llorona*! The weeping woman! Or stung by the scorpion! Or —

TELÉMACA: My *papá* will come home!

ROSAMARIA: When?

BLANCA: How?

TELÉMACA: I don't know. I don't know!

(TELÉMACA throws her basket of corn toward them in frustration. The few ears of corn scatter.)

ROSAMARIA: *(Insultingly.) This* is the daughter of Omero?!

(ROSAMARIA and BLANCA exit haughtily. TELÉMACA sinks to her knees. TOMÁS enters and sees her sitting amidst the scattered corn.)

TOMÁS: Telémaca, what has happened? Your maíz —

TELÉMACA: Has *Papá* not come home because of me?

Because I have not kept his land as he would want it?
Is he ashamed of me?

(TELÉMACA begins to cry.)

TOMÁS: Don't cry, my friend.
TELÉMACA: I will cry forever . . . like *La Llorona*.
TOMÁS: *(Frightened.)* Do not speak of her. It's almost
    night!
TELÉMACA: Let her come for me. I will say: "Find my
    papá. He is lost, like your children!"
TOMÁS: Omero is not lost.
TELÉMACA: Then where is he?

(TOMÁS has no answer.)

TELÉMACA: I will find him.
TOMÁS: What?
TELÉMACA: I will find my father. Before it is too late.
TOMÁS: But —
TELÉMACA: Do not say a word to anyone, especially
    Mamá. I will leave tonight. Pray for me.
TOMÁS: May you find him and return.
TELÉMACA: And may you, my friend, have better luck
    selling my corn. *Adios*, Tomás.

(TELÉMACA leaves. TOMÁS remains.)

End of Scene

To help you with the language and culture in the scene:

Pueblo: Means "village" in this scene
Pan dulce: Means "sweet cakes"
Maiz: Means "corn"
La Llorona: A ghost from Mexican legend who wanders the
    night, crying, searching for her lost children. Parents
    sometimes frighten their children into going to sleep at
    night or warn them not to go out into the night alone
    because of *La Llorona.*
Adios: Means "good-bye."

Quien Busca, halla means
"He who searches, finds." or "He who seeks will find a
    way."

CHAPTER SIX

Scenes for Groups

(7 – 20 minutes)

HONEST

Adapted from *What Part Will I Play?*

CHARACTERS: (13 w, ages 12 - 14)
    Brittany
    Tiffany
    Erica
    Enid
    Mike
    Zora
    Karina
    Marley
    Jessie
    Amy
    Frances
    Desiree
    Chase
    Stage Manager (offstage voice)

SETTING:
    An empty stage in a theater

    What Part Will I Play? *is a play that gives voice to middle school girls' hopes, fears and failures, fantasies and hard knocks. The girls arrive at a theater to audition for a promising new play. Each girl has come with her own ambitions, dreams, even secrets. But the girls learn that the director will be late. So the stage manager announces that they must first do improvisations — all part of the auditioning process.*

STAGE MANAGER *(Offstage voice.)*: OK, girls. Everybody's clear about improvisations, right?

AMY: They're a kind of drama game.

MIKE: It's like doing a play without a script. They can be so funny. I am such a clown in improvisations —

MARLEY: Save it, Mike.

MIKE: OK, no problem.

BRITTANY: Look. You decide who you are, where you are, and what's going on in the scene. *(Looking at all the other girls.)* Even beginning actors know that.

STAGE MANAGER *(Offstage voice.)*: Who's first?

(BRITTANY crosses quickly downstage. AMY and JESSIE catch up.)

STAGE MANAGER *(Offstage voice.)*: Terrific. Now, imagine that you are three girls at a party. What we are looking for here, girls, is honesty, OK? Begin.

BRITTANY: I am so glad that you could come to my party.

AMY: Oh, so am I.

JESSIE: So am I.

BRITTANY: We've got dancing —

AMY: Great food.

BRITTANY: Lots of food.

JESSIE: Parties are great place for food.

(Spotlight on JESSIE. All other characters freeze. We hear the thoughts in her head.)

JESSIE: I can't believe I said that. I'm such an idiot! I'm not sure what to say when I'm in front of people in real life, much less when I'm pretending to be somebody.

(Lights restore back to improvisation.)

BRITTANY: How funny. Boy, you're the life of the party.
JESSIE: Thanks.
AMY: So, what's *your* favorite color?

(Spotlight on AMY. All other characters freeze.)

AMY: Where did *that* come from? Everybody here will think I'm the worst actress in the world. I just came to this audition because my mom thought I'd make some new friends. Nobody will even want to *talk* to me after this.

(Lights restore back to improvisation.)

BRITTANY: Purple.
JESSE: *(Overlapping with BRITTANY.)* Yellow.
BRITTANY: *Bright* purple.
AMY: Yeah. *(Under her breath.)* Sorry.
BRITTANY: That's OK.

(Spotlight on BRITTANY. All other characters freeze.)

BRITTANY: Here I am again. Trying to make a good impression so I can get the lead so I can become a famous actress so I can move to New York and get away from these people!! . . . and my parents.

(LIGHTS and MUSIC with a driving beat signal a full transition to a fantasy that now includes all the girls.)

JESSIE: Isn't this a great party?

ALL: He said honest.

JESSIE: I don't know what I'm doing up here!

ALL: Honest!

AMY: What does he expect of me?

ALL: Honest!

BRITTANY: I've got to prove something. Don't get in my way.

ALL: *Honest!!!*

(In groups of three, the girls come quickly downstage and assume the position of one of the three girls in the improvisation, saying what they would be thinking if they were up there. Each is frozen before and after her line.)

ERICA: What is he thinking? What does he want? I don't want to pretend to be like somebody else. *(Looking at TIFFANY.)* Except maybe like her.

TIFFANY: There's got to be a part for me. I *must* be perfect for something. I'm always perfect. I think.

DESIREE: I want this part so bad I can taste it. I always finish second place. Not this time.

CHASE: This time feels like all the other times I've tried to be in a play. I don't look like anybody else. I don't act like anybody else. Why would anybody want to give me a part?

FRANCIS: No one can take this away from me. I'll just keep acting like I know everything. I *do*, don't I?

MIKE: Do they think I'm funny? They've got to think I'm funny. I don't know how to be any other way. What can I say next?

KARINA: Nobody here is like me. What are they thinking about me? I bet they hate me already.

ENID: I should have stayed at the library. They were going to have a party with cupcakes and fruit punch. I really blew it.

MARLEY: This auditioning is nothing different than what happens every day. Put on a mask. Play a part. Pretend.

ZORA: This is a weird space to be in. So much pressure to *be* something. I don't know what I am. Why should I? I'm *twelve*!

ALL: You don't know?

ERICA, DESIREE, and TIFFANY: What part you want?

CHASE, FRANCIS, and MIKE: Who you want to be?

KARINA, MARLEY, and ENID: What you want to be when you grow up?

ALL: Who you are??!!

ZORA: Not really.

MIKE: Then it's time for you to audition for the rest of your life.

(The fantasy continues as Game Show Music begins. The girls pick up ZORA and place her on top of a cube. MIKE and CHASE are co-hosts. TIFFANY and DESIREE play the "Vanna White" roles. Other girls are contestants and spectators. The whole sequence is played as a broad parody, but the contestants respond honestly.)

CHASE: Thank you and welcome to our show. Let's say hello to our first contestant.

(Cheers and applause. ZORA is still confused.)

MIKE: Today is your chance to win —
CHASE: From a full selection of choices —

MIKE: The role you want to play for the rest of your life.

ZORA: But —

MIKE: First we need to ask you a few qualifying questions.

CHASE: Do you want to play the lead in this world or some lousy little part where nobody notices you?

ZORA: I —

MIKE: Do you want a career, success, and lots of money?

ZORA: I think I —

CHASE: Do you want a leading man?

ZORA: Sure.

MIKE and CHASE: Sounds like you want it all!

ZORA: I just want to be happy.

MIKE and CHASE: Happy??!!

(Buzzer sounds.)

TIFFANY: Wrong choice.

DESIREE: Too corny!

CHASE: Next.

ERICA: *(Stepping forward.)* Let me play. I want to be a lawyer.

CHASE: Now you're talking.

MIKE: Let's take a peek behind the career door and see what's in store for our lovely contestant number two.

(BRITTANY, FRANCIS, and JESSIE create the "career door" through mechanical movements.)

DOOR: Money!

ERICA: Great.

DOOR: Success!

ERICA: Great!

DOOR: Law school.

ERICA: Oh. That's OK. I think I'm smart enough.

DOOR: Start studying now. Take the right courses in school. Pre-law everything. Make the right friends. Go to the right parties. Don't waste time!

ERICA: But I'm only in junior high!

MIKE: Gotta choose your part *now!*

ERICA: But what about my dance class?

CHASE: Forget it. You're thirteen! Got to start early if you want a leading role. Next!

AMY: I want to audition for a mother part.

MIKE: You're not very ambitious, are you.

AMY: I think I'd be a good mom. I want to have kids.

(A group creates crying and kid-fighting noises.)

AMY: *(Not so sure now.)* I think.

CHASE: Gotta want more than *that* to be a modern woman.

TIFFANY: You've got to want to get ahead.

DESIREE: You've got to go for it, baby.

CHASE: Next!

(Buzzer sounds.)

MARLEY: Go for what? I feel like I'm auditioning every day — at home, at school, for a different part, a different future.

CHASE: How else are you supposed to feel between the developmental ages of twelve and sixteen, hmmm??

MARLEY: But what are the parts? What's the play?

MIKE and CHASE: *Life* young lady. What part will *you* play?

KARINA: I just want a better part than I have now. I want more friends.

MIKE: So what's the problem? Just go out there and make a few.

KARINA: I don't know how! How do you choose friends? How do they choose you?

CHASE: It's all part of the game.

KARINA: I don't know how to play!

(Buzzer sounds.)

CHASE: Next!

FRANCIS: I want an important part.

BRITTANY: I want a new part.

MARLEY: I want my own part!

ENID: I want a different part!

ALL: Just let me play the lead!!

(Music becomes upbeat as each girl crosses eagerly down stage. Each is confident, speaking her dreams.)

ZORA: I know I can show him who I really am.

MARLEY: I want a part. For the first time.

ENID: Maybe there *is* a place for me here.

KARINA: For me! That'd be incredible!

MIKE: I could stay on stage forever.

FRANCIS: All the attention!

DESIREE: The spotlight! That's all I need.

TIFFANY: The applause!

AMY: The lights. It's magic.

JESSIE: Magic!

BRITTANY: Just let me perform. Then I'm on top of the world.

ALL: On top of the world!

(All girls repeat their lines excitedly as they return to the pre-fantasy positions with JESSIE, BRITTANY, and AMY downstage in the improvisation. All freeze. Music out. Lights back to reality — the improvisation.)

BRITTANY: So, wanna try a little caviar?
JESSIE: Uh, yeah. Pass the Doritos.
AMY: Sure.
STAGE MANAGER *(Offstage voice.):* Thank you, girls. Next.

End of Scene

A QUICK MIDSUMMER

CHARACTERS: (8 w, 6 m, ages 11 - 13)
- Phoebe (Peter Quince)
- Nathan (Bottom)
- Sharleen (Hermia)
- Zuri (Flute)
- Amanda (Egeus)
- Minori (Puck)
- Dominic (Oberon)
- Darren (Demetrius)
- Tevon (Theseus)
- Eve (Hippolyta)
- Dayo (Lysander)
- Lexy (Titania)
- Gaiya (First Fairy)
- Hannah (Helena)

SETTING:
A middle school English classroom

A group of middle school students have been charged with telling the story of Shakespeare's A Midsummer Night's Dream *in ten minutes or less. The students, the characters they are playing and the plot of the play share some fun similarities in this scene. [These students have devised their scene so that the actors remain in character even when they are narrating.]*

PHOEBE: Would everybody *please* sit down? We've got to rehearse our *Midsummer Night's Dream!*

NATHAN: Dost thou think just becauseth you're Peter Quince in the play that you are in chargeth?

SHARLEEN: That is *so* fake Shakespeare.

NATHAN: *(To SHARLEEN.)* A pox upon you, thou foul-breathed lily-livered rabbit sucker!

PHOEBE: Nathan, we're not playing the Shakespearean insult game right now!

ZURI: Aw, that's the best!

AMANDA: She *said* not now!

PHOEBE: Minori, stop running around the room.

MINORI: I've got to be fast. Puck puts spells on everybody.

DOMINIC: Not yet. I'll tell you when.

AMANDA: Phoebe's the president of drama club, so she's the director. Those are the rules.

SHARLEEN: Whose rules?

AMANDA: My rules.

DARREN: Amanda, the rule queen!

TEVON: Hey, I'm student council president. That gives me rank.

EVE: *(To TEVON.)* You just like to *think* you're in charge.

DOMINIC: Well, I've got it over everybody. I'm the *king*.

DAYO: Yeah. Of the fairies!

(This gets a laugh from everybody, the boys especially.)

DOMINIC: So! The rest of you are mere mortals. I'm a supernatural king!

LEXY: There's a queen, too, Dominic. Or are you hogging the spotlight —

LEXY and GAIYA: As usual.

DOMINIC: Hey, I know who's most important, that's all.

LEXY: Exactly. *Me.*

PHOEBE: Guys! Mrs. Dawes is expecting us to present this next period.

NATHAN: Then give us our parts.

SHARLEEN: We know who we're playing.

HANNAH: Yeah. Darren gets to be rude to me onstage now, as well as off.

SHARLEEN: *(To HANNAH.)* Like I can help it that he likes *me* instead of *you*?

HANNAH: He didn't used to.

NATHAN: You know, Phoebe, I can play more parts than what you've given me.

ZURI: You've already got the best part.

MINORI: It's perfect for you — Bottom, the biggest donkey in the class. Hee-haw!

NATHAN: I could do the whole play as a one-man show. How about it?

(Big groan from the rest of the group.)

ZURI: He'd do great!

DARREN: Zuri just doesn't want to play a girl!

ZURI: Yeah, why *do* I have to play a boy that plays a girl? Why can't a girl be Flute?

PHOEBE: That's what makes it funny.

NATHAN: I'll say all the lines and the rest of you can act it out while I talk, like a mime show.

LEXY: No way.

DOMINIC: Who's hogging the spotlight now?

LEXY: Just stay on your side of the room, Dominic. Come on, Gaiya.

GAIYA: Coming and *happily*.

MINORI: There goes the queen and her follower!

GAIYA: At least I don't mess everything up in the play like you! Putting the spell on the wrong guy!

MINORI: It's a comedy!

NATHAN: We could do tragedy instead. *Hamlet* or *Macbeth!* I could play those parts, too.

TEVON: Nathan, you are Bottom.

PHOEBE: *Just* Bottom. OK.

NATHAN: *(After a dramatic pause.)* Your loss.

PHOEBE: Now. *(Handing out scripts.)* I've printed out scripts for everybody. It's just how we've been practicing, but I wrote it all down.

AMANDA: *(Looking at NATHAN.)* So *no one* would make stuff up on the spot.

PHOEBE: I put all the Shakespeare in quotes.

DOMINIC: Wouldn't want to confuse it with how people *really* talk.

EVE: Shakespeare is beautiful!

ZURI: When you understand it.

HANNAH, LEXY, and SHARLEEN: And *we* understand it.

ZURI: *(Sarcastic.)* Girls are *so* perfect!

PHOEBE: *(Referring to the script.)* I might be a copy or two short.

HANNAH: Want to share with me, Darren?

DARREN: I'll share with Sharleen.

DAYO: I'm sharing with Sharleen.

AMANDA: Only two people can share.

SHARLEEN: *(Smugly.)* Sorry, Darren.

DARREN: I know my lines, anyway.

HANNAH: Fine.

(MINORI takes the plastic flower she is holding and whacks DARREN on the head with it.)

MINORI: Zap!

PHOEBE: Not yet, Minori!

MINORI: I'm getting into character!

DAYO: *(To DARREN.)* Should we practice our sword fight?

DARREN: Yeah. Get the swords.

PHOEBE: No —

(The following lines come fast, almost overlapping, as PHOEBE struggles to get people on task.)

LEXY: Why can't I sing? In the real play Titania sings —

EVE: What does an Amazon warrior wear to her wedding?

AMANDA: Are we going to be timed? We can't go a second over ten minutes!

GAIYA: If I'm the first fairy, where's the second?

ZURI: *(Looking at the script.)* Hey, I barely get to talk.

NATHAN: I can be a fairy, too —

PHOEBE: *Quiet!*

(Everybody settles down.)

PHOEBE: Look, do we want our scene to go to the regional drama finals or not?

TEVON: Relax, Phoebe. We got it, right guys? Places everybody.

PHOEBE: Fine! For the top!

(Everybody takes a place on the edge of the playing space. PHOEBE steps forward.)

PHOEBE: That's more like it. OK —

NATHAN: I thought I got the first line.

LEXY: We all do!

AMANDA: That's fair.
PHOEBE: Watch for my cue.

(Everybody does. She cues them.)

ALL: On a magical midsummer night —

(MINORI and GAIYA cross onstage as Puck and the First Fairy.)

MINORI: The fairy kingdom buzzes with the news that Oberon and Titania will soon meet in the moonlit forest. "How now, spirit! Whither wander you?"
GAIYA: "Over hill, over dale!" But the fairies fear that their King and Queen will fight, because Titania has refused to give Oberon a small boy to be his servant. "Farewell, thou lob of spirits. I'll be gone. Our queen and all our elves come here anon."
MINORI: "The king doth keep his revels here to-night. Take heed the queen come not within his sight."

(DOMINIC and LEXY cross onstage as Oberon and Titania.)

NATHAN *(To PHOEBE.):* This is when they fight, right?
PHOEBE: Shhhhh!
DOMINIC: "Ill met by moonlight, proud Titania."
LEXY: "What, jealous Oberon?" Come.
DOMINIC: "Give me that boy, and I will go with thee."
LEXY: *(Furious.)* "Not for thy fairy kingdom!"

(LEXY turns and storms off, followed by GAIYA.)

DOMINIC: "Well, go thy way: thou shalt not from this grove till I torment thee for this injury." *(He storms off in the other direction.)*

MINORI: *(Ad-libbing.)* Score one for Dominic!

PHOEBE: Minori! Offstage! Go!

MINORI: "See how I go, swifter than an arrow from Cupid's bow."

(MINORI exits. PHOEBE cues TEVON and EVE.)

TEVON: But in the court of the Duke of Athens, all is celebration! Duke Theseus will wed the beautiful Hippolyta tomorrow. *(To EVE.)* "I woo'd thee with my sword, and won thy love, doing thee injuries. But I will wed thee in another key, with pomp, triumph and with reveling."

EVE: But soon a nobleman arrives with his daughter Hermia and two boys.

(Enter AMANDA, SHARLEEN, DARREN, and DAYO.)

AMANDA: "Full of vexation come I with complaint against my child, my daughter Hermia. Stand forth, Demetrius. My noble lord, this man hath my consent to marry her. Stand forth, Lysander. This man hath bewitched the bosom of my child."

(ZURI giggles.)

LEXY and GAIYA: Grow up!

SHARLEEN: Hermia begs to marry Lysander, the boy she loves, rather than Demetrius, the boy her father has chosen for her. "I would my father looked but with my eyes."

DOMINIC: "Rather your eyes must with his judgment look."

AMANDA: *(The rule-queen.)* See!

DARREN: "Relent, sweet Hermia: and Lysander, yield thy crazed title to my certain right."

DAYO: "You have her father's love, Demetrius; Let me have Hermia's: do you marry him."

ZURI: *(Not in the script.)* Besides, Hannah likes Darren and he used to like her, till he dumped her for Sharleen.

PHOEBE: Shhhhh!

ZURI: It's true!

HANNAH: *(To SHARLEEN.)* "O, teach me how you look, and with what art you sway the motion of Demetrius' heart."

SHARLEEN: *(To HANNAH, not in the script.)* I don't do anything! He just likes me. *(Back to the script.)* Hermia begs the Duke to bend the law of Athens and allow each girl to marry whom she chooses!

TEVON: But the Duke says no!

AMANDA: *(Triumphantly.)* Ha!

(All exit but DAYO and SHARLEEN.)

DAYO: "Ay me! The course of true love never did run smooth."

SHARLEEN: What are we going to do??

DAYO: "Hermia, if thou lovest me, steal forth thy father's house to-morrow night!"

SHARLEEN: "To-morrow truly will I meet with thee."

DAYO: So Lysander and Hermia run off into the woods!

SHARLEEN: Planning to escape and marry secretly.

(SHARLEEN and DAYO exit. It is NATHAN's cue but he is so wrapped up in watching that he misses his cue.)

PHOEBE: Nathan. Nathan! Go!

NATHAN: Oh. *(He enters.)* On this same night, a group of workers from the town prepare a play to perform at the Duke's wedding.

(PHOEBE and ZURI join NATHAN onstage.)

PHOEBE: "Here is the scroll of every man's name, which is thought fit through all Athens to play in our interlude before the duke and the duchess on his wedding-day at night. You, Nick Bottom, are set down for Pyramus."

NATHAN: "What is Pyramus? A lover or a tyrant?"

PHOEBE: "A lover, that kills himself most gallant for love."

NATHAN: "That will ask some tears in the true performing of it!" *(Not in script.)* I can cry like a thunderstorm! Wanna see?

PHOEBE: *(Not in script.)* Nathan! *(Back to the script.)* "Francis Flute, the bellows-mender."

ZURI: "Here, Peter Quince."

PHOEBE: "Flute, you must take Thisby on you."

ZURI: "What is Thisby? A wandering knight?"

PHOEBE: "It is the lady that Pyramus must love."

ZURI: "Nay, faith, let me not play a woman; I have a beard coming."

DOMINIC: *(Not in script.)* In your dreams!

ZURI: *(Not in script.)* Lay off!

PHOEBE: "You shall play it in a mask, and you may speak as small as you will."

ZURI: Fine.

NATHAN: We will meet and rehearse most courageously. "Take pains; be perfect: adieu."

(PHOEBE, NATHAN, and ZURI exit.)

PHOEBE: *(Not in script.)* Enter Puck!

(PHOEBE enters, followed by DOMINIC.)

MINORI: That same night in the forest, the mischief-maker Puck comes when his master Oberon calls. Oberon is planning a trick to play on his queen.
DOMINIC: "Fetch me that flower; the herb I showed thee once: The juice of it on sleeping eye-lids laid will make a man or woman madly dote upon the next live creature that it sees."
MINORI: So Titania will love whatever she sees first when she wakes up?
DOMINIC: May she wake "when some vile thing is near!"

(DOMINIC exits.)

MINORI: Puck finds the flower, but then stops when he comes upon four love-sick mortals in the woods.

(HANNAH chases DARREN across the stage.)

HANNAH: Helena has told Demetrius of Hermia and Lysander's flight, hoping that he will love her again. But Demetrius wants only Hermia.
DARREN: "Tempt not too much the hatred of my spirit; For I am sick when I do look on thee."
HANNAH: "And I am sick when I look not on you."

(HANNAH and DARREN run off, as DAYO runs on.)

MINORI: Oberon has asked Puck to enchant Demetrius, too. But by mistake, Puck puts the spell on Lysander.

(MINORI puts the flower-spell on DAYO.)

DOMINIC: *(Entering.)* So Oberon has to place the love spell on Demetrius.

(DARREN runs back on and DOMINIC enchants him. HANNAH runs on.)

MINORI: When the boys wake up, they *both* see Helena first! Now both boys love Helena!

(Both boys swoon over HANNAH.)

HANNAH: *(Amazed.)* What is going on?!
MINORI: "Lord what fools these mortals be!"
SHARLEEN: *(Entering.)* Poor Hermia cannot understand why Lysander no longer loves her!
HANNAH: And Helena is sure that Hermia and the boys are all just trying to make a fool of her!
DARREN: *(To HANNAH.)* "I say I love thee more than he can do."
DAYO: *(To DARREN.)* "If thou say so, withdraw, and prove it too."
DARREN and DAYO: *(Not in script.)* Sword fight!
NATHAN: *(Not in script.)* Yes!!!
PHOEBE: *(Not in script.)* Offstage!

(DARREN and DAYO rush off.)

SHARLEEN: Hermia is furious at Helena for stealing her Lysander!

HANNAH: Your hands are quicker than mine for a fray, "My legs are longer though, to run away."

(HANNAH runs off.)

SHARLEEN: "I am amazed, and know not what to say."

(SHARLEEN runs off. PHOEBE, NATHAN, and ZURI enter.)

MINORI: Then the mischief-maker Puck spies Nick Bottom and his friends rehearsing their play. Seeing that Nick Bottom acts his part no better than a donkey would, Puck puts a spell on Bottom that turns him into an ass!

NATHAN: Hee-haw! "If I were fair, Thisby, I were only thine."

ZURI: "O monstrous! O strange!"

PHOEBE: "We are haunted. Pray, masters! Fly, masters! Help!"

NATHAN: Hee-haw! Hee-Haw!

GAIYA: Bottom's loud braying frightens away his friends and awakens the enchanted fairy queen.

LEXY: "What angel wakes me from my flowery bed?"

NATHAN: Hee-haw!

LEXY: Titania falls instantly in love with Bottom the donkey.

MINORI: *(Not in the script.)* I *love* this part.

LEXY: "O, how I love thee! How I dote on thee!"

NATHAN: Hee-haw!

DOMINIC: *(Entering.)* But Oberon makes Puck take the spell off Lysander.

MINORI: *(Not in script.)* Do I have to?
DOMINIC: *(Not in script.)* Yes!
MINORI: OK.

*(MINORI "magically" draws HANNAH, SHARLEEN,
DAYO, and DARREN onstage and puts them "to sleep.")*

MINORI: "Jack shall have Jill, all shall be well."

(Enter TEVON, EVE, and AMANDA.)

TEVON: As dawn breaks, the Duke and his bride welcome
their wedding day by hunting in the woods.
EVE: But they discover Lysander, Hermia, Helena, and
Demetrius are all there asleep!
AMANDA: "My lord, this is my daughter here asleep; And
this, Lysander; this Demetrius is; This Helena. I wonder
of their being here together." Hermia's father wants to
punish them!
TEVON: But the Duke waits to hear their story.
SHARLEEN: Hermia, Helena, and the boys awake —
DAYO: But they remember very little of the confusion of
the night before.
DARREN: All Demetrius knows is that he loves Helena!
HANNAH: Really?
DARREN: I do!
HANNAH: Most wonderful!
SHARLEEN: And Lysander again loves his Hermia.
DAYO: I do!
SHARLEEN: They beg the Duke to be allowed to marry
their true loves.
TEVON: "Egeus, I will overbear your will; For in the temple
by and by with us these couples shall eternally be knit."

EVE: Join us and be married to whom you love this night.

ZURI: *(Not in the script.)* Does Pyramus get to marry Thisby?

PHOEBE: *(Not in the script.)* Nope. They both die.

NATHAN: *(Not in the script.)* Like Romeo and Juliet!

ZURI: *(Not in the script.)* Cool.

(All three couples exit. DOMINIC and LEXY enter.)

DOMINIC: Oberon begins to pity Titania, so he lifts the spell from her eyes.

LEXY: Oberon, "what visions have I seen! Methought I was enamoured of an ass!"

NATHAN: *(Not in the script.)* You were!

DOMINIC: All is forgiven between the king and queen.

LEXY: Harmony returns to the fairy kingdom.

DOMINIC: "Come, my queen, take hands with me, and rock the ground whereon these sleepers be. Hand in hand, with fairy grace, will we sing and bless this place."

(DOMINIC and LEXY exit. MINORI and NATHAN enter.)

MINORI: *(Not in the script.)* Although she doesn't want to . . . *(Back in script.)* Puck changes Bottom back into a man.

(NATHAN spins around and is a man again. But he doesn't speak.)

PHOEBE: Nathan, you talk now.

(NATHAN is lost in the wonder of this magic moment

of the play. He delivers his lines not as the show-off, but very truthfully, honestly.)

NATHAN: "Methought I was . . . Methought I had . . ."
Bottom wonders if what he remembers from the night before — his long ears and the love of the fairy queen — was perhaps all just a midsummer night's dream.

(The kids are impressed by this honest moment from NATHAN. Then the whole cast enters.)

MINORI: If we shadows have offended,
Think but this, and all is mended,
DOMINIC: That you have but slumbered here
While these visions did appear.
EVE: And this weak and idle theme,
No more yielding but a dream,
ZURI: Gentles, do not reprehend:
GAIYA: if you pardon, we will mend:
MINORI: Else the Puck a liar call;
TEVON: So, good night unto you all.
EVE: Give me your hands, if we be friends,
ALL: And Robin shall restore amends.
NATHAN: Behold the future champions of the regional drama festival!

(A big cheer from the whole group.)

PHOEBE: Places, again, for the top!

(All the students excitedly return to their places.)

End of Scene

A DRAGON!

Adapted from *The Reluctant Dragon*

CHARACTERS: (4 w, 4 m)
    Glaston: 10
    Woolchester: 14
    Darby: 12
    Kendal: 14
    Morpeth: 13
    Grimbsy: 12
    Finchley: 13
    Verity: 12

SETTING:
    In a village square in Medieval England

Rumors are flying among the villagers about a dragon who has been seen upon the Downs (hills above the town). GLASTON is a big fan of dragons. He has read all about them in his books. In fact, he has adventured up to meet the dragon and discovered that he is a very nice fellow. GLASTON's brother, WOOLCHESTER, is petrified of the beast, but his sister, DARBY, tries to understand GLASTON's point of view. The rest of the young villagers are completely set in their ideas of what a dragon is like. DARBY worries that the prejudice against all dragons could spell doom for GLASTON's newfound friend. The young people have gathered to make a plan to rid their village of the dragon. The scene begins with everyone talking at once.

ALL: *(Repeating/ overlapping lines/ ad-libbing/ all talking at once.)* It's true!/ I've seen him!/ Where?/ He was in the cave!/ He was beside the cave!/ He's green!/ He's blue!/ He charged me!/ Are you *sure?*

KENDAL: Order! Order everyone! Let Morpeth speak.

MORPETH: I speak the truth, I tell you. I've seen him.

VERITY: Me, too!

DARBY: *(Doubtful.)* Have you indeed.

MORPETH: He's got big bulging eyes —

GRIMSBY: And fangs!

DARBY: When did *you* see him, Grimsby?

KENDAL: Let him speak.

GRIMSBY: Well, I didn't exactly, but I know he's got fangs!

VERITY: Pointy fangs!

MORPETH: With edges sharp as daggers!

WOOLCHESTER: And our sheep. They're disappearing, I tell you.

DARBY: Are you sure, brother?

WOOLCHESTER: I'll wager all the shillings in Sussex they are!

FINCHLEY: That's because the dragon just leans back and sucks in a huge great breath, and all the sheep within miles go flying down his throat!

GRIMSBY: Cows and horses, too!

VERITY: Cows and horses!

KENDAL: Aye! When a dragon lives above your village, everything goes awry!

MORPETH: The milk's gone sour and the bread won't rise. We'll be starving soon for sure.

DARBY: *(Sarcastically.)* Is that why we have nothing to eat but your meat pies? How many did you sell in the market today, Morpeth?

GRIMSBY: I'd sooner loose me teeth than eat one of her meat pies.

MORPETH: Then trot off and slay the dragon, "Squire" Grimsby. You were boasting that you could.

VERITY: Aye, you said you could!

GRIMSBY: Then I will.

(Everyone waits expectantly.)

GRIMSBY: *(Backing off.)* In . . . my own time.

(The group erupts into arguments, but KENDAL quickly silences them.)

KENDAL: Order! Now, it is clear that we should most probably *kill* this beast.

VERITY: Kill him!

KENDAL: But how, exactly?

DARBY: Can't we just shoo the dragon off. Our brother Glaston says —

WOOLCHESTER: *(Quieting his sister.)* Nothing! He says nothing at all.

MORPETH: We'll need weapons!

VERITY: Lots of weapons.

KENDAL: But strategies first.

FINCHLEY: How about poison spears?

GRIMSBY: Spears with spikes!

FINCHLEY: Spikes with poison!

GRIMSBY: Aye, spikes with poison! Let me at that dragon!

WOOLCHESTER: Charge on then, Sir Grimsby.

GRIMSBY: But . . . I'm not charging by myself!

(The group erupts into arguments again, but MOR-PETH tops them.)

MORPETH: What, are we cowards?

FINCHLEY: Never.

VERITY: Never!

FINCHLEY: *(To VERITY.)* I *said* that already!

MORPETH: Then, brave villagers of Guildemere! *(She begins a chant.)* We soon should attack, with spear or with ax, the dragon that lives upon the Downs.

DARBY: But —

ALL (but DARBY): *(Joining in the chant.)* We soon should attack, with spear or with ax, the dragon that lives upon the Downs. We soon should attack, with spear or with ax, the dragon that lives upon the Downs!

GLASTON: *(Entering.)* What's going on?

DARBY: Glaston —

GRIMSBY: *(Thrusting a weapon into GLASTON's hand.)* Aye, *Glaston* can lead the charge against the beast.

GLASTON: What?

FINCHLEY: You love reading about battles, Glaston. Now you've got a real one.

GLASTON: Against the dragon? But there's no need —

KENDAL: Quiet, Glaston. We're working out something important here. So, Squire Grimsby —

GRIMSBY: Who?

FINCHLEY: You!

GRIMSBY: Right. Me.

KENDAL: You say one must pierce a dragon.

GRIMSBY: Right dead in the heart . . . I think.

KENDAL: Then what?

GLASTON: But Kendal —

MORPETH: You have to make sure it confesses all of its wicked, evil deeds.

GLASTON: If I might interrupt —

KENDAL: Would someone silence their little brother?!

DARBY: But you should listen, Kendal! Glaston's been . . . well, he's been . . .

(All eyes are on DARBY.)

DARBY: Well . . . sort of passing a few afternoons with the beast.

ALL: *What??!!!*

WOOLCHESTER: Just a few, mind you.

DARBY: Glaston's ever so knowledgeable of such beasts.

GLASTON: Thank you, sister. Now, this particular dragon is very unusual —

MORPETH: Look at his eyes. The dragon's curse might be upon him.

VERITY: The dragon's curse!

GLASTON: Nonsense.

FINCHLEY: *(Taking a closer look at GLASTON.)* Aye, he's hexed.

VERITY: Hexed!

MORPETH: Hexed, by the dragon's evil eye.

(ALL but DARBY spit twice through their fingers onto the ground, a symbol of warding off a curse.)

WOOLCHESTER: Are you hexed, brother?

GLASTON: I shouldn't think so.

GRIMSBY: Hang a clove of garlic around his neck.

KENDAL: Fetch a mirrored shield.

FINCHLEY: Leave a pitcher of milk outside your cottage at night. That will ward him off.

GLASTON: This dragon is actually very nice. You can't help liking him. Why, I'm quite sure he would enjoy having each of you for supper.

(ALL react in terror.)

GLASTON: I didn't mean eat *you*!

GRIMSBY: I'll be no meal for a beast!

MORPETH: We know what to do with a dragon, don't we!

VERITY: Don't we! *(To KENDAL.)* Do we?

GLASTON: Listen! Please —

GRIMSBY: I'll meet him on the Downs, I will, lance in hand and pierce him through the heart myself!

(ALL cheer except DARBY. Angered that the other young people won't listen to him, GLASTON decides to feed the fire of their fears.)

GLASTON: Will you, "Squire" Grimsby. Oh, I'd be careful if I were you. There's poison in a dragon's blood.

VERITY: Poison?

GLASTON: And when you stab him, the poison can travel all the way up your spear and poison *you*. And your horse, too!

GRIMSBY: He's hexed alright!

GLASTON: *(To FINCHELY.)* And milk! Why, this dragon loves milk. He drinks it by the gallon, making his wings grow bigger and *bigger*!

MORPETH: Get away, devil!

DARBY: *(Confused by his behavior.)* Are you hexed, brother?

(GLASTON whirls around and winks quickly at his sister, then whirls back to the group.)

GLASTON: Your only hope is to learn my secret charm to keep dragons away.

KENDAL: Tell us.

FINCHLEY: Quickly!

VERITY: Quick!

GLASTON: If, when you first see the moon at night, you turn round three times and whistle quite loudly, then you'll be safe from harm.

MORPETH: Whistle?!

GLASTON: Remember! *(Stalking them like a fearful dragon.)* He has big, bat-like wings!

(ALL but DARBY back away from him slowly.)

GLASTON: And poison in his blood.

(GRIMSBY is the first to burst into a whistle. Then all whistle and turn in three circles, fearfully as they exit. But DARBY stops WOOLCHESTER. He now realizes that GLASTON has been playing a trick.)

GLASTON: Remember! When you first see the moon.

KENDAL, VERITY, GRIMSBY, FINCHELY, and MORPETH: *(Running off in horror.)* Ahhhhhhh!!!

(GLASTON laughs heartily.)

GLASTON: They believed me.

WOOLCHESTER: That was wicked, Glaston.

GLASTON: But they're being so silly about dragons —

DARBY: I'd warn that dragon friend of yours, brother. It won't be long before they come up with a plan to rid our village of the beast. A plan that will work!

WOOLCHESTER: He'll be warning no dragon, friend or no. He's not spending another spilt minute with that beast.

GLASTON: But Woolchester —

WOOLCHESTER: I'm the oldest, and I forbid you to go near that dragon's cave again.

GLASTON: But we were going to have tea tomorrow.

WOOLCHESTER: Tea? With a dragon?!

GLASTON: He makes ever so nice sandwiches, too.

DARBY: Let him go back, Woolchester. Just once.

WOOLCHESTER: No!

GLASTON: But the dragon will be so lonely.

WOOLCHESTER: Break my heart! That's what a dragon deserves, if you ask me.

GLASTON: How do you know? You've never met him.

WOOLCHESTER: I *know* about dragons.

DARBY: Do you?

GLASTON: Not *this* dragon.

WOOLCHESTER: Come along, Glaston.

GLASTON: But —

WOOLCHESTER: I said. Come along. You, too, Darby.

DARBY: Yes brother.

(WOOLCHESTER turns to exit. DARBY and GLASTON dutifully follow. But behind his big brother's back, GLASTON looks at DARBY hopefully. She motions for him to run off the other way. GLASTON happily does. WOOLCHESTER does not see. DARBY smiles and follows WOOLCHESTER off.)

End of Scene

A BATTLE OF THE GODS

A Myth from Ancient Egypt

CHARACTERS: (3 w, 4 m, chorus of 4 or more w or m)
    A Chorus
    Geb: god of the earth
    Isis: queen of the earth
    Horus: son of Isis
    Bast: the cat goddess
    Sobek: the crocodile god
    Seth: god of chaos

SETTING:
    The time of myth in the ancient world

All cultures have sought to explain events in the natural world through their stories and myths. The origin of earthquakes is the subject of this myth from ancient Egypt. It is a battle between the powers of light (HORUS) and darkness (SETH) — a battle that the god of Earth (GEB) finds very amusing. [The chorus are active participants in the storytelling, creating with their bodies the mountains, the river, the boats, etc.]

CHORUS: Geb was the god of the Earth.

GEB: I bend my knees and the mountains are formed. I crook my elbow and valleys are born.

ISIS: Yes, Geb, we've heard all that before. Tell instead how I am far more worshipped than you.

GEB: Well you *are* the mother goddess. The queen of all
    earth —
ISIS: Go on.
GEB: All adore Isis, the feminine spirit — the life force! Is
    that enough?
ISIS: You could add, "From Isis, all life flows."

(HORUS enters.)

GEB: Including my grandson! Welcome, Horus.
ISIS: You are looking very fit and strong, my son.
GEB: What adventure do you have in store for yourself
    today?
HORUS: I'm preparing for a great contest.
GEB: Oh no, not that again.
ISIS: Horus, you must not challenge Seth to any more con-
    tests.
HORUS: But he has challenged me. He claims that he is the
    rightful ruler of all Egypt.
GEB: I thought Seth learned his lesson when Ra changed
    you into a shining bird.
HORUS: And I swooped down in victory upon Seth and his
    army!
GEB: That was a good one!
ISIS: No, Seth will never be satisfied until all of our king-
    dom is his.
HORUS: All of it should be mine! My father was Osiris!
GEB: Spoken like the true son of his parents!
ISIS: You must be careful, son. Seth is the god of chaos. Of
    confusion! No doubt he will try to trick you.
GEB: Seth never plays fair, it's true.
ISIS: It is far too dangerous, Horus. I will not allow it.
GEB: But consider, Isis. If Horus does not challenge Seth,

our whole kingdom could be swallowed in Seth's darkness.

BAST: Geb is right, great Isis. Once Seth turned his whole army into crocodiles and hippopotami so they could hide from Osiris underwater.

SOBEK: I thought that was very clever.

BAST: Of course you would, Sobek. You're the god of crocodiles.

SOBEK: At least you should appreciate Seth's sneakiness, Bast. You, the sneakiest of cat goddesses.

BAST: *(At SOBEK.)* Hisssss!

SETH: *(Entering, overhearing.)* Yes, the crocodile trick was indeed one of my finest moments in battle.

GEB: Greetings, Seth. I would say you are welcome here, but you are not.

SETH: I do not intend to stay long. I am here merely to see if Horus has accepted my challenge.

ISIS: Never!

HORUS: I'm not afraid, Mother. For my father's sake, let me try.

ISIS: *(Giving in.)* May my power be with you.

GEB: And mine.

SETH: He will need it.

HORUS: What are your terms, Uncle?

SETH: Accept the challenge first, then hear the terms.

BAST: Careful, Horus.

SOBEK: *(To BAST.)* He will trick him. Watch!

SETH: You must do whatever I ask.

HORUS: I accept.

SETH: Excellent. I challenge you to a race. A race down the Nile.

HORUS: That's no challenge. I will easily win.

SETH: In boats of stone.

GEB: That's impossible!

ISIS: I forbid it.

SETH: Too late.

SOBEK: How can a boat of stone float?

SETH: Perhaps you have lost the challenge before you have begun.

HORUS: Not so fast, Uncle. Meet me on the banks of the Nile just before the sun sets. I will meet your challenge.

SETH: Very well. I look forward to watching you drown.

(SETH exits.)

ISIS: Horus, don't be foolish.

HORUS: I have a plan, Mother. And I will win.

(HORUS exits. The CHORUS reassembles as ISIS and GEB assume a place to watch the contest. HORUS enters on one side of the Nile with BAST and SOBEK. SETH enters on the other side. CHORUS members create the boat and the river.)

CHORUS: At sunset, Horus came to the banks of the Nile with a boat made of the lightest wood. But he had covered it with clay so it appeared to be made of the heaviest stone.

HORUS: Where's your boat, Uncle? If I sail alone, I win.

SETH: You will *sink* alone.

HORUS: Will I? Come Bast. Sobek. Help me launch my boat.

BAST: Yes, Horus.

SOBEK: With pleasure.

SETH: Good-bye, Nephew. Forever!

(HORUS slips into the Nile in his boat. It floats.)

HORUS: See you at the finish line!
SETH: Stone can float??!!
BAST: You'd best hurry, Seth.
SOBEK: Before you lose.
SETH: Quickly, Geb. Give me stone from one of your
    mountains so I, too, may have a magic boat.
GEB: If you insist.

(GEB gestures and a boat appears for SETH.)

ISIS: Hurry, Seth. You wouldn't want Horus to get there
    first.

(SETH leaps into the boat.)

BAST and SOBEK: Smooth sailing!

(The boat quickly sinks.)

SETH: AHHHHH!

*(SETH is covered by the water and disappears.
HORUS comes back on shore.)*

BAST: You've won, Horus.
HORUS: For now, at least.
ISIS: Clever boy!
GEB: Clever ruler of all Egypt!
SOBEK: If you ever need a crocodile army, Lord Horus, I
    will be proud to serve.

HORUS: Thank you, Sobek. Will you serve me as well, Bast?

BAST: With great honor. Purrrr!

GEB: *(Beginning to laugh.)* Isis, did you see Seth's face when he saw Horus' boat?

(GEB lets out a big laugh and the earth starts to shake.)

HORUS: What's happening?

ISIS: Careful, Geb. You mustn't laugh.

GEB: I can't help it.

(With GEB's next burst of laughter, the earth quakes even more.)

ALL: Ahhh!

ISIS: You are the ground, the mountains, and the valleys. When you laugh —

(GEB lets out another big laugh and everyone almost rocks to the ground.)

ALL: The earth quakes!

(The earth continues to rumble and gods and people tumble as GEB laughs.)

ISIS: My son. Your first test as pharaoh will be to restore order to all of Egypt.

HORUS: I will, Mother. Grandfather, please!

(GEB stops laughing. The earth ceases to rumble.)

GEB: Sorry.
HORUS: Rise, Egypt. Your Pharaoh has spoken.

(All characters now become the Chorus.)

CHORUS: Horus ruled wisely and well. Hereafter, all
    pharaohs were very careful not to make Geb laugh.

End of Scene

HOW JACK GOT A JOB

Adapted from *Sing Down the Moon: Appalachian Wonder Tales*

CHARACTERS: (15, flexible w or m)
Storyteller One
Storyteller Two
Storyteller Three
Jack
Lucy
Will
Tom
Store Owner
Farmer
Farmer's Wife
Cow
Puppy
Rich Man
Daughter
Donkey

SETTING:
In the mountains of Appalachia

Sing Down the Moon: Appalachian Wonder Tales celebrates the rich culture and humor of the mountain folks of Appalachia. Their stories came from England and Ireland, but changed in their telling through the generations. There are many "Jack Tales" about the

*boy who may not be the smartest sibling, but who usu-
ally wins in the end.*

*The storytellers in this scene should not stand outside
of the action, but become a part of it — becoming the
creek, the haystack, or a slamming door. And when
the characters are narrating about themselves, they
should not step out and be a narrator. They should
still be that character in the moment they are describ-
ing.*

*The scene begins with the hapless Jack racing on,
stumbling over his own feet. He plays around balanc-
ing on a log as his family enters.*

STORYTELLER ONE: Once upon a while ago, Jack and his
    sister Lucy, and his brothers Will and Tom, lived on a
    farm a ways out from town. Now, Will and Tom helped
    out the best they knew how, but Jack! He wasn't
    worth —
LUCY: *(Interrupting her sweeping.)* Diddly-squat.
TOM: *(To his siblings.)* Jack doesn't know how to make up
    a bed or wash a dish.
WILL: He can't cook or iron or chop wood.
TOM: He can't even milk a cow!
LUCY: Nope.
STORYTELLER ONE: Well, one day, Jack said to his sister:
JACK: Lucy, I wanna get a job so I can make me some
    money.
LUCY: Jack, you can't do anything! How do you think you
    can get you a job?
JACK: I don't know. But I will!

(JACK sets off.)

STORYTELLER ONE: So Jack headed to town.
STORYTELLER TWO: He went from one store to the other.
    But every time, the same thing happened.
JACK: I'm lookin' for a job.
STORE OWNER: What can you do?
JACK: Nothin'!

(STORE OWNER slams door in JACK's face.)

STORYTELLER TWO: Jack got mighty discouraged and
    was headed back home when he got an idea.
JACK: I'm gonna try one more time.
STORYTELLER TWO: Jack stopped at the first farmhouse
    he came to and walked up bold as brass to the door.
FARMER: *(Entering.)* Hello, son. What can we do you for?
JACK: I'm lookin' for a job.
WIFE: What can you do?
JACK: Anything!
FARMER: That farmer —
WIFE: And his wife —
FARMER: *(Handing JACK a rake.)* Offered Jack a job on
    the spot.
STORYTELLER THREE: It was the fall of the year, so Jack
    went to raking up leaves.

(JACK doesn't know what to do with the rake.)

FARMER: Hold it this way, son.
JACK: Oh. *(JACK rakes.)*
STORYTELLER THREE: It was hard work! *(JACK col-
lapses.)* Jack got plum tuckered out.

FARMER: Looks like you're done, Jack.

JACK: I am?

FARMER: Now you get paid.

JACK: I do?

FARMER: Here's a quarter.

JACK: I'm gonna be rich!

(JACK starts off for home.)

STORYTELLER ONE: Jack was so happy that he was throwing that quarter up in the air and catching it as it came back down. Then he came to a foot log over a creek. He was crossin' and tossin' —

(SPLASH is heard as JACK watches the coin fall in the water.)

STORYTELLER ONE: When he dropped that quarter right into the creek.

JACK: Good thing I'm going back to work tomorrow. I'll get paid all over again.

(LUCY enters to meet JACK.)

LUCY: *(Entering.)* Jack, did you find you a job?

JACK: Sure did and I got paid!

LUCY: Well, who'd a-thunk it. Let me see your money, Jack.

JACK: Well . . .

STORYTELLER ONE: Jack had to tell her about his creek crossing.

LUCY: What good is getting a job if you go and throw your pay in the creek! When you go back tomorrow, don't throw your pay up in the air, Jack. Put it straight in your pocket.

JACK: All right, Lucy.

(LUCY exits.)

STORYTELLER TWO: The next day, Jack headed back to work. On his way, he came up on the rich man's big fancy house.

(RICH MAN enters and JACK admires him and his house from afar.)

RICH MAN: It was two floors high, with a porch running all around so you could look clear down the valley.

JACK: One of these days, I'm gonna have me a house just like that.

STORYTELLER TWO: But right now, Jack needed to get to work.

FARMER: *(Tossing JACK a shovel.)* To help the farmer clean his cow barn.

COW: *(Entering.)* Moooo.

JACK: Yes, sir.

STORYTELLER TWO: It took Jack a long time —

COW: *(With attitude.)* Moooo!

STORYTELLER TWO: Cause he tried to hold his nose with one hand and his shovel with the other.

COW: Mooooo!!!

STORYTELLER TWO: But pretty soon, he finished up.

JACK: Is it time for me to get paid?

FARMER: Got your pay right here, Jack — a bottle of fresh milk.

JACK: Thank ye, sir!

STORYTELLER THREE: Jack turned his footsteps toward home, but then he remembered what his sister had said.

JACK: "Don't throw your pay in the air, Jack. Put it straight in your pocket."

STORYTELLER THREE: Jack twisted his pants around to get good aim on his pocket and he started pouring.

(JACK pours the milk into his pocket.)

JACK: This pocket's plum full and I still got more to go.

STORYTELLER THREE: Well the milk didn't rightly stay where it was poured.

JACK: Look at there. Now I got more room.

STORYTELLER THREE: Jack walked on home with milk a-sloshin' and squishin' from his belly to his toes.

(LUCY and TOM enter to meet JACK.)

LUCY: Jack! What'd you get paid?

TOM: Another quarter?

JACK: Nah, I got a whole bottle full of milk. I put it right straight in my pocket — hey, where'd that milk go?

LUCY: Jack, why'd you pour the milk in your pocket?!

JACK: You told me to! "Don't throw it in the air. Put it straight in your pocket."

TOM: She was talking about money, not milk!

LUCY: Are you going back to work tomorrow, Jack?

JACK: Reckon so.

LUCY: If you get money, put it in your pocket. But anything else will already be in what you're supposed to carry it in. Leave it where he puts it.

TOM: You got that?

JACK: Sure do.

(LUCY and TOM exit and JACK heads back to work.)

STORYTELLER ONE: The next day was butter-churning day at the Farmer's house. Jack managed to do most of the churning.

(JACK struggles with the butter churn. WIFE has to help him out.)

WIFE: The wife put the butter into stone crocks that she dipped into cool water in the springhouse.
JACK: 'Bout time for me to get paid?
WIFE: I've got you a big ball of butter, Jack. Now, give me your hat.
JACK: Yes, ma'am.
WIFE: I'll line your hat with leaves and put the butter right in it.

(WIFE hands the hat, with leaves shading the butter, to JACK.)

WIFE: You hurry on home so that butter won't melt.
JACK: Thank ye!

(JACK starts off for home but he stops.)

STORYTELLER TWO: But it's hard to run carrying a heavy old hat.
JACK: I'll just put my hat where it's supposed to be so I can swing my arms when I run.
STORYTELLER TWO: Well, the day was hot as fire and as

soon as Jack put that hat on, the butter started to melt. Through every hair on his head! Round his ears! By the time Jack got home, he was buttered head to toe. His sister took one look at him —

(LUCY and WILL enter to meet JACK.)

LUCY: All I need now is a big biscuit to roll you around on so I can get some of that butter back! Now, why did you do that?

JACK: You told me to leave whatever they give in whatever they give it. That's what I did.

TOM: Don't you know how to keep butter cold?

JACK: You dip it down in cold water.

LUCY: So when you're walking home and your pay gets soft, you just dip it in the creek.

TOM: Can you remember that till tomorrow at least?

JACK: Sure I can.

(LUCY and TOM exit.)

STORYTELLER THREE: The next day, Jack headed back to the farmer's to work the hay.

(FARMER tosses JACK a pitchfork.)

WIFE: Why Jack, that haystack is big enough to last us all winter.

FARMER: He's getting a might better at his job. Let's give him something special. Here, doggie.

(FARMER whistles and a puppy runs on.)

PUPPY: Yip. Yip.
JACK: A puppy!
PUPPY: Woof!
WIFE: You take good care of the little fella.
JACK: I will! Come on, pup!

(JACK heads for home with the puppy.)

JACK: "Don't throw it in the air . . . don't put it in your
    pocket . . . don't carry it under your hat." I'll just carry
    it under my arm. Hold up. This puppy's getting pretty
    warm and soft. What did Lucy say? If you're walking
    home and your pay gets soft . . .
PUPPY: Yip?
STORYTELLER ONE: Reckon you know what Jack did. He
    took that puppy down and dipped it right in the creek.
    By the time Jack got home, that puppy was blowing
    creek-water bubbles out its nose.

(Enter LUCY, WILL, and TOM to meet JACK.)

LUCY: Jack. Were ya tryin' to drown your pay?
JACK: I just did what you said.
TOM: Don't you know how to bring a puppy home?
JACK: Reckon not.
LUCY: You take this cord and you put it round his neck!
WILL: Aw, just give him the sack, Lucy.
LUCY: *(Handing him a sack.)* Now you listen, Jack. Take
    this empty flour sack, and whatever the farmer gives
    you —
WILL: *Except* a puppy!
LUCY: You put it in here and carry it home on your back.
TOM: You got that?

JACK: Put it in the sack. Carry it on my back. Bye.

(LUCY, WILL, and TOM exit.)

STORYTELLER TWO: The next day, when Jack started back to the farmer's, he couldn't help but look up again at the rich man's beautiful house.

(DAUGHTER and RICH MAN enter.)

JACK: Sitting in the window was the rich man's daughter. She was the prettiest thing Jack had ever seen.

DAUGHTER: *(Crying.)* But she was crying like she'd never stop.

STORYTELLER TWO: Poor thing lost her mother two winters back, and hadn't smiled or laughed from that day to this.

RICH MAN: Whoever can get my daughter to cease her crying, I will give him two wagonloads of gold.

JACK: Jack started dreaming 'bout what he'd do with all that gold!

FARMER: Jack!

JACK: But right now, Jack had to get back to his job.

(FARMER and WIFE enter with DONKEY.)

FARMER: Jack, you've been working for us a whole week. We wanna give you something that can help you get home, if you work it right.

DONKEY: Hee-Haw!

JACK: I ain't never had a donkey!

WIFE: Well now you do.

DONKEY: Hee-Haw!

(JACK heads off home, but the donkey is stubborn. He does not budge.)

JACK: Come on, donkey. What did Lucy say?? "Put it in the sack. Carry it in on your back!"

STORYTELLER THREE: Well, Jack tried to sack that donkey by the tail. *(DONKEY won't let him.)* Then by the feet. *(DONKEY tries to kick him.)* Finally, he put that sack as fast as it'd go down over the donkey's head.

DONKEY: Hee-Haw!!

STORYTELLER THREE: Well, that donkey couldn't see and couldn't half breathe.

JACK: Reckon that's it for the sack. Now I gotta get it on my back.

STORYTELLER THREE: Jack tried to pick the donkey up every which a way. Finally he crawled right under him, stuck his head between the donkey's front legs, then stood right up.

STORYTELLER ONE: Now here was Jack, huffin' and puffin,' and the donkey hee-hawin'.

DONKEY: Hee-Haw!!

STORYTELLER TWO: It was the funniest, fool sight you ever saw.

DONKEY: Hee-Haw!!

STORYTELLER THREE: Just then, the rich man's daughter came out on her fancy porch and spotted poor Jack and his donkey.

(DAUGHTER bursts out laughing.)

STORYTELLER ONE: She laughed and laughed till she thought her sides would split.

RICH MAN: Jack, you must be the smartest boy in the world.

JACK: Huh?

RICH MAN: A blindfolded singing donkey riding up the road on the back of a boy. How'd you ever think of something so funny!

(RICH MAN tosses JACK a big sack of gold.)

RICH MAN: The rich man gave Jack two wagonloads of gold. Stay a spell if you like.

DAUGHTER: *(Giggling. Flirting.)* Hi Jack.

JACK: Jack gave serious thought to staying, but he reckoned he ought to get on home.

STORYTELLER TWO: Now Jack had all the money he needed.

LUCY *(Delighted.)*: And a donkey.

DONKEY: Hee-Haw!

LUCY and JACK: So he never had to get a job again.

(All the characters from the story enter to join JACK, LUCY, and the DONKEY in an exuberant dance that ends with JACK throwing gold coins into the audience.)

End of Story

Sources

The following monologues, listed by chapter and cited by character name, were based on characters in my plays listed below.

CHAPTER ONE
Monologues for Young Women

> Frances, *What Part Will I Play?*
> Katie, *Blessings*
> Telémaca, *The Odyssey of Telémaca*
> Ariadne, *Lift: Icarus and Me*
> Atalanta, *Lift: Icarus and Me*

CHAPTER TWO
Monologues for Young Men

> Trey, *Spirit Shall Fly*
> Jack, *Sing Down the Moon: Appalachian Wonder Tales*
> Lenny, *Lift: Icarus and Me*
> Sandy, *A Perfect Balance*
> Glaston, *The Reluctant Dragon*

CHAPTER THREE
Monologues for Young Women or Young Men

> Klaus, *The Sorcerer's Apprentice*

The following scenes, listed by chapter and cited by title, were adapted from or inspired by scenes in my plays listed below.

CHAPTER FOUR
Scenes for Two Actors

"Over the Rainbow," *Broken Rainbows*
"Playing to be Heard," *Broken Rainbows*
"The Quest," *Perseus Bayou*
"Lying Spirit Cat," *Perseus Bayou*
"Tiger in a Trap," *Dancing Solo*
"Real, Like Me?" *Mississippi Pinocchio*
"What Do You Know, Pinocchio," *Mississippi Pinocchio*
"Happy Landing," *Lift: Icarus and Me*
"See Where You Land," *Lift: Icarus and Me*
"For My Father," *The Odyssey of Telémaca*

CHAPTER FIVE
Scenes for Four Actors

"The Audition," *What Part Will I Play?*
"Quien Busca, Halla" (He Who Searches, Finds), *The Odyssey of Telémaca*

CHAPTER SIX
Scenes for Groups

"Honest," *What Part Will I Play?*
"A Dragon!" *The Reluctant Dragon*
"How Jack Got a Job," *Sing Down the Moon: Appalachian Wonder Tales*

Play Bibliography

Blessings The play is available for reading in *Most Valuable Player and Four Other All-Star Plays for Middle and High School Audiences,* published by Smith and Kraus, Inc. Publishers. 888.282.2881. www.smithandkraus.com. All inquiries regarding the performance rights should be addressed to Mary Hall Surface, 2023 Rosemont Ave NW, Washington, D.C. 20010, Phone/fax: 202.232.5397. MHSurface@aol.com.

Broken Rainbows The play is available for reading in *Most Valuable Player and Four Other All-Star Plays for Middle and High School Audiences,* published by Smith and Kraus, Inc. Publishers. 888.282.2881. www.smithandkraus.com. All inquiries regarding the performance rights should be addressed to Mary Hall Surface, 2023 Rosemont Ave NW, Washington, D.C. 20010, Phone/fax: 202.232.5397. MHSurface@aol.com.

Dancing Solo The play is available for reading in *Most Valuable Player and Four Other All-Star Plays for Middle and High School Audiences,* published by Smith and Kraus, Inc. Publishers. 888.282.2881. www.smithandkraus.com. And from Dramatic Publishing, P.O. Box 129, Woodstock, IL 60098. Phone: 800.448.7469. www.dramaticpublishing.com. All inquires regarding performance rights should be addressed to Dramatic Publishing.

Lift: Icarus and Me Book by Mary Hall Surface, Lyrics by David Maddox and Mary Hall Surface, Music by David Maddox. The play is available for reading and performance rights from Mary Hall Surface, 2023 Rosemont Ave. NW, Washington, DC, 20010, Phone/fax: 202.232.5397. MHSurface@aol.com. See www.williebellmusic.com for more information.

Mississippi Pinocchio Book by Mary Hall Surface, Lyrics by David Maddox and Mary Hall Surface, Music by David Maddox. The play is available for reading and performance rights from Dramatic Publishing, P.O. Box 129, Woodstock, IL 60098. Phone: 800.448.7469. www.dramaticpublishing.com. All inquires regarding performance rights should be addressed to Dramatic Publishing. See www.williebellmusic.com for more information.

The Odyssey of Telémaca Book by Mary Hall Surface, Lyrics by David Maddox and Mary Hall Surface, Music by David Maddox. The play is available for reading and performance rights from Mary Hall Surface, 2023 Rosemont Ave. NW, Washington, DC, 20010, Phone/fax: 202.232.5397. MHSurface@aol.com. The award-winning original cast recording is available from numerous on-line sources, including Amazon.com. See www.williebellmusic.com for more information.

A Perfect Balance The play is available for reading and performance rights from Mary Hall Surface, 2023 Rosemont Ave. NW, Washington, DC, 20010, Phone/fax: 202.232.5397. MHSurface@aol.com. See www.schoolsculptures.com for more information.

Perseus Bayou Book by Mary Hall Surface, Lyrics by David Maddox and Mary Hall Surface, Music by David Maddox. The play is available for reading and performance rights from Dramatic Publishing, P.O. Box 129, Woodstock, IL 60098. Phone: 800.448.7469. www.dramaticpublishing.com. All inquires regarding performance rights should be addressed to Dramatic Publishing. The award-winning original cast recording is available from numerous on-line sources, including Amazon.com. See www.williebellmusic.com for more information.

The Reluctant Dragon The play is available for reading and performance rights from Anchorage Press Plays, 617 Baxter Ave., Louisville, KY, 40204. Phone/Fax: 502.583.2288. www.applays.com.

Sing Down the Moon: Appalachian Wonder Tales Book by Mary Hall Surface, Lyrics by Mary Hall Surface and David Maddox, Music by David Maddox. The play is available for reading and performance rights from Dramatic Publishing, P.O. Box 129, Woodstock, IL 60098. Phone: 800.448.7469. www.dramaticpublishing.com. All inquires regarding performance rights should be addressed to Dramatic Publishing. The award-winning original cast recording is available from numerous on-line sources, including Amazon.com. See www.williebellmusic.com for more information.

Spirit Shall Fly The play is available for reading and performance rights from Mary Hall Surface, 2023 Rosemont Ave. NW, Washington, DC, 20010. Phone/fax: 202.232.5397, MHSurface@aol.com.

The Sorcerer's Apprentice The play is available for reading and performance rights from Anchorage Press Plays, 617 Baxter Ave., Louisville, KY, 40204. Phone/Fax: 502.583.2288. www.applays.com.

What Part Will I Play? The Play is available for reading and performance rights from Mary Hall Surface, 2023 Rosemont Ave NW, Washington, D.C. 20010, Phone/fax: 202.232.5397, MHSurface@aol.com.

MARY HALL SURFACE is an internationally acclaimed playwright, director, and producer of theater for young audiences and families. Her work has been presented at the Kennedy Center, Seattle Children's Theatre, the Smithsonian, England's Carpe Diem Theatre, and at international festivals in Canada, Sweden, Germany, Taiwan, Japan, Scotland, Ireland, and France. She is the recipient of the Charlotte Chorpenning Cup from the American Alliance for Theatre and Education for an outstanding body of work and of the Aurand Harris Fellowship from the Children's Theatre Foundation for professional excellence. She was the vice-president of the U.S. Center for the International Association of Theater for Children and Young People (ASSITES/USA) for seven years and is an on-site evaluator for the National Endowment for the Arts. She provides professional development for teachers through the Kennedy Center and presents writing residencies throughout the United States in schools and in communities.

Smith and Kraus, Inc.
Plays, Monologues, and Scenes for Grades 7–12

If you require prepublication information about upcoming Smith and Kraus books, you
may receive our semiannual catalogue, free of charge, by sending your name and address
to *Smith and Kraus Catalogue, 4 Lower Mill Road, North Stratford, NH 03590. Or call us
at (888) 282-2881, fax (603) 643-1831. SmithandKraus.com.*